HARLOT'S MOON

HARLOT'S MOON

Ed Gorman

HEADLINE
FEATURE

First published in Great Britain in 1997
by HEADLINE BOOK PUBLISHING

A HEADLINE FEATURE hardback

10 9 8 7 6 5 4 3 2 1

British Library Cataloguing in Publication Data

Gorman, Edward
  Harlot's moon
  1.Serial murderers - Psychology - Fiction
  2.Detective and mystery stories
  I.Title
  831.5'4[F]

ISBN 0 7472 1684 3

Typeset by
Letterpart Limited, Reigate, Surrey

Printed and bound in Great Britain by
Mackays of Chatham PLC, Chatham, Kent

HEADLINE BOOK PUBLISHING
A division of Hodder Headline PLC
338 Euston Road
London NW1 3BH

To Tom Spaight – in lieu of the six million dollars I mooched off him in our college days.

Injustice, suave, erect, and unconfined,
Sweeps the wide earth, and tramples o'er mankind –
While prayers to heal her wrongs move slow behind.

Iliad, Homer

1:

POLICE DEPARTMENT

Tawanna Lucilee Jackson
Age: 23
Race: African-American
Occupation: Prostitute
Marital Status: Single
Military Service: None

Jackson: I'll tell you one thing, sweetheart, they sure ain't never gonna forget Tawanna. First thing after I got the phone call about my HIV test comin' back positive the second time . . . you know what I did, babe? I hit the streets. Absa-fuckin-lutely, like Cherie used to say before she went and died of AIDS a couple years ago. Absa-fuckin-lutely. You know what I'm sayin'? All these white johns that think they're so high and mighty, pullin' up in their big cars and tryin' to impress me an' all . . . They're gonna remember Tawanna, I can promise you that. Just like Cherie, babe, they'll start runnin' this fever and havin' this scratchy throat all the time and they'll go to the doctor . . . They ain't ever gonna forget Tawanna, no way. I do me two, three johns a night for the next few years . . . that's an awful lot of fancy white ladies see their lives go to shit the same way my mama and me saw OUR lives go to shit . . . No, sir, they never gonna forget ol' Tawanna.

Tawanna Jackson

So one night when she's thirteen, Tawanna decides to give it a try for herself. She waits till after eight, till her mother's done some dope and is sleeping in the bedroom.

She walks downtown. A lot of these businessmen, they work real late. She knows she looks a lot older than her years. At least that's what people always tell her.

Her sister Gayla's been doing this for three years now and that's how she can afford the five-year-old Chevrolet and her own apartment over in Wennington Heights and getting her hair fixed up all the time over at the Sassy Lady.

So now it's Tawanna's turn. Technically, she's a student in ninth grade but she knows this isn't going to last much longer. School bores the shit out of her. Anyway, who needs schoolin' for somethin' like this, just do what comes natural girl, that's all, just do what comes natural.

She's wearing a tan T-shirt and no bra, her young breasts outlined beautifully against the tan cotton, and white shorts so tight you can see the shape of her sex.

Plus she's done what her older sister once told her to do.

'There's three places a man wants a girl to put perfume, Tawanna, on your neck, and on your breasts and down between your legs.' Tawanna has never forgotten this . . .

Night in downtown Cedar Rapids, hot July night, sodium vapor lights and lights in some of the offices in some of the taller buildings; smells of heat and exhaust fumes and the

5

closeby river, teenagers out in their cars radios booming tires squealing; a road show at the Paramount, line around the block, mostly white folks wearing summer shirts and skirts and talking that way that white folks do. Lots of laughing, which Tawanna envies and resents. She laughs a lot too, she supposes, but she never sounds this *happy* when she laughs.

Over the next hour, Tawanna pretty much covers the downtown. The only attention she attracts is from teenage boys, farm boys especially. Hot nights like this, they come from all the little towns around Cedar Rapids. They pretend they're real hip and shit but they're not. They see a girl and all they can do is giggle like little kids.

There is a park in the center of town and that's where she ends up, hot and tired and frustrated. She figured this would be pretty easy. She even stole a condom from her mother's drawer. All ready. For nothing.

She is just getting up when she sees the shiny red sports car pull up to the curb across from the bench where she's sitting.

Gray-haired guy gets out, tall, lanky kind of guy, gray summer-weight suit on, and comes over to her.

'I'm looking for a little fun tonight,' he says. 'How about you?'

'Cost you.'

'How much?'

'Hundred bucks.'

He laughs. Actually, he's got a nice, gentle laugh.

'That's a little steep.'

'I'm a virgin.' As, technically, she is. The one boy who was ever inside her was Randy from down the block and he was so swacked on crack, he couldn't quite get it up enough to get it all the way in.

'How about fifty?'

'Seventy-five.'

'Sixty,' he says.

Sixty is so much more money than she's ever had . . .

They drive out along the river. You can see the lights of

house boats in the dark summer night . . .

'How old're you?'

'Twenty,' she says.

That oddly tender laugh again.

'Now tell me how old you are really?'

'Eighteen.'

He smiles at her. 'I could get in trouble.'

She smiles back. 'So could I.'

The weird thing, and the thing she really likes, is that she feels in control of the situation. Here's she with this older white guy who's got this fancy sports car . . . and she's in control.

They get out past the boat docks then, and out past the point where the river suddenly turns north, and he aims his little red car up into the hills, and the state park.

He pulls over by a pavilion and punches off the headlights.

Night in the country: owlcry and star-blessed sky and distant dog bark and silver moonlight on long grasses waving in the sudden and blessed breeze.

And that's when she hears the odd *snicking* sound and looks over to see that he's just opened a very long pearl-handled switchblade, the point of which he puts against her throat.

He travels the blade down from her throat to her left breast, where the point lingers against her nipple, and then continues on down to her sex.

'You scared?'

'God, mister, please.'

Now he don't even *look* like the same guy. Or sound the same, either.

Then he takes her hand and guides it to his groin.

The knife point goes back to her throat.

'Please, mister,' she says. 'Please.'

'Do me,' he says. 'Do me.'

What choice does she have?

And all the time she's doing him, he keeps the knife point pushed right against the side of her neck.

★　★　★

When it's all over, he takes the knife and puts it in the glove compartment.

'You really got scared, didn't you?' he says.

She doesn't say anything. She's pissed off, she's frightened, and suddenly she's very, very weary. No thirteen-year-old in the history of the world has ever been so weary.

'Hey,' he says, 'I want us to be friends.'

She glares over at him. He's crazy. Like most white folks.

He laughs his laugh. 'I wasn't really going to hurt you. It's just how I get off. I mean, I can't even get it up unless I'm pretending that I'm going to hurt the girl I'm with. But I wouldn't actually do anything. I really wouldn't.'

And the weird thing is, she believes him. He's his old nice-guy self again and she believes him.

'You really scared me.'

He puts a paternal hand on her shoulder. 'Tell you what, how about if I make it a hundred for tonight?'

'Wow. Are you kidding?'

'Nope. A hundred dollars it is.'

She's thinking of all the stuff she can buy with a hundred dollars. She'll go to the Sassy Lady and get her hair fixed for sure.

He takes out his billfold and pulls out a crisp new bill and hands it to her.

'I was just having my fun,' he says. 'I didn't mean to scare you that much. You forgive me?'

She looks at the hundred-dollar bill and says, 'Yeah, yeah I do.'

He reaches out a long, slender white hand and they shake. 'Friends?'

She giggles. 'Yeah. Friends.'

That night, Tawanna decided that her sister's profession was a lot better than going to school. A whole lot better.

One

i

In the morning, the first thing she said was, 'I'm going to try very hard not to be depressed today.'

'Good for you,' I said.

We were both in my large double bed in the apartment I keep in Cedar Rapids. I spend some of my time in a small country town forty miles west. But these days I worked for a law firm as an investigator so I'd brought my shaving kit, my three cats and several packages of new white jockey shorts along. You can never be too rich, too thin or own too many pairs of jockey shorts. At least if you're baching it, you can't. Saves on a lot of unnecessary trips to the laundry in the basement.

'I mean it's raining, and I feel like I may be getting a head cold but I don't care. I'm not going to be depressed.'

'I'm proud of you.'

'I'm not even going to think about Frank this morning,' she said.

'That's the way to do it.'

'You don't give a damn about any of this, do you? You'll say anything to shut me up. You won't even tell me the truth about my buns when I ask you, will you?'

'Oh God,' I said, 'not the buns thing. It's too early in the morning.'

Felice is a woman I met at a seminar I spoke at last year.

9

She attended because the subject of psychological profiling, which I did during my years with the FBI and which I now do for law firms and police departments who need specialized help from time to time, interested her. She hadn't enrolled in college. She just attended seminars.

You can take her the wrong way, Felice, and a lot of people do. They see the doe-eyed beauty and the reckless poise, and they hear all about the money, and they think she's a cream-puff. But they don't bother to see the sorrow. Two bad marriages, with her being cheated in all meanings of that word by both husbands. Nor do they see the neurotic, alcoholic parents who raised her. Or the three miscarriages that ultimately landed her in a mental hospital up in Dubuque. Every few months she tries some new anti-depressant but none of them ever work very well for her. She's walked down some long, hard road, Felice has.

Lately, she's become obsessed with her buns. This started about a month ago when she went up to the mall to try on swimsuits for summer and happened to get a glimpse of her bottom in a four-way mirror.

'I'm going to walk over to the window, all right? And you watch my buns as I walk, okay?'

I sighed. 'All right.'

'And be honest now.'

'Of course.'

'You bastard. You really don't care about this, do you?' She was genuinely on the verge of tears.

'God, look, Felice, I like your buns. Just the way they are, I mean.'

'And how are they?'

'How are they what?'

'They're drooping, aren't they? That's what you're afraid to tell me, aren't you?'

'They aren't drooping.'

'Then they're sliding.'

'They aren't drooping and they aren't sliding, either.'

'You're sure?'

She stood at the head of the bed completely naked, her backside to me, her fetching face in profile over her shoulder. Her flesh would be nice and soft and she would smell wonderfully of sleep. I liked her butt, I liked her arms, I liked her ears, I liked her elbows, and I liked every other part of her, too. I especially liked her soul. For all her self-absorption, she was one of the sweetest, most tender women I'd ever known.

Then she smiled. 'God, I can't believe I'm doing this again. Can you? The buns thing, I mean. All the poor people who don't have anything to eat and all the poor people in mental hospitals and all the poor people dying of some terrible disease – and I'm whining about my butt.'

'You said it. I didn't.'

'I don't know how you can stand me. You're such an . . . adult, Robert. You really are. And I'm – I'm—'

She apparently couldn't find a word derogatory enough.

The six-unit apartment house sits on a shelf of rock above the Cedar River. On sunny days you can see half a mile upriver, to the first bend where the speed boats race on Sundays. Now the windows were hard gray and dirty with city rain. Rain has a tyrannical effect on Felice's moods. Fortunately, her bad moods are sometimes tempered by her sense of irony. As now, when she suddenly realized that the buns thing was getting tiresome.

The phone rang.

She smiled at me. She has a lovely damned smile. She really does. 'I'm tired of talking about my buns. How about talking about my left breast?'

'I think I'd rather talk about your right one, if you don't mind. We always talk about your left one.'

She laughed. 'I'm sorry I started in on the buns thing, Robert. I really am. Do you think they offer night-school courses in how to be an adult?'

That's the other thing about Felice. She apologizes like the morning-after drunk who destroyed your living room the night before.

I picked up on the fourth ring.

The funny thing was even though I had seen him only sporadically over the past fifteen years, I recognized his voice immediately.

'Robert Payne?'

'Hey, Father Gray. How are you?'

'You don't have to call me "Father," Robert. You know that.'

Steve Gray and I had grown up in the same rural town where I still kept the house where Kathy and I had lived, Kathy being my young wife who'd died of an aneurysm four years earlier. Steve had always been the jock and I'd always been the book reader. I'd been a more likely candidate for the priesthood than him. He'd had plenty of girls, had put away more than his share of teenage beer, and had even smoked a few illicit joints in his time. He went to the University of Iowa for two years, made the first-string JV football squad, and then suddenly transferred to the seminary in Dubuque. His beloved father had died of cancer over a grim two-year period. During that time, Steve drove back home from college every chance he got.

Watching his father die had changed Steve. He suddenly understood the 'idea' of Jesus Christ, he'd explained to me one beery night a few years back. Even if you didn't believe that Christ was divine, you had to believe in the compassion and dignity of His words, Steve said. So Steve became a priest. He was now a Monsignor, and a very young Monsignor, at St Mallory's here in Cedar Rapids.

I suppose we distrust the kind of religious calling Steve got. We're too cynical about such things. Some people really do want to live their lives helping others.

The last time I'd spoken to Steve I'd asked him if he could give me a general dispensation for sins such as fornication and masturbation but he said he didn't think he could do stuff like that. Not and keep his Roman collar anyway.

'It's great to hear your voice, Steve.'

A hesitation. 'Robert, I need to ask you a favor and if you

don't want to do it, I'll certainly understand. It may be . . .
illegal.'

'What's the favor, Steve?'

Felice was watching me carefully. The word 'Father' had
gripped her attention.

'I'd like you to come to the Palms Motel.'

'Out on 49?'

'Right.'

'Come now, you mean?'

'Yes. But I need to tell you the rest of it.'

'All right.'

'There's a dead man in the room.'

'I see.'

'A priest. He worked with me at St Mallory's.'

'Don't say anything more on the phone. I'm working for
lawyers in a murder case and the other side may have
bugged this phone.'

'They really do things like that?'

'They really do things like that.' I swung my legs off the
bed. 'What's the room number?'

'154. Ground level. Around back.'

'I'll be there in twenty minutes.'

'Is it illegal, you coming out here this way?'

'Probably. But I'm not going to worry about that right now.'

'I really appreciate it, Robert.'

When I got off the phone and stood up, Felice said, 'You'll
want to take the first shower.'

'Thank you, honey – that would be helpful.'

She stood there lusciously naked, hip-switched, her sweet
face that of a little girl who wants to ask her father a question
but is afraid to.

'You probably don't want to talk about it, do you?'

'The phone call?'

'Yeah.'

'I don't know much more than that there's a dead priest in
a motel room.'

'God. A dead priest. Wow.'

All the time we talked, I grabbed socks and underwear and shirt and slacks and tie.

She came over and touched my arm. 'I'm sorry about my butt. For bugging you about it, I mean.'

I kissed her quickly. 'I'm not sorry about it. In fact, I'm very happy about it. You have a wonderful butt. A *glorious* butt.'

'Honest?'

'Honest.'

'You're nice.' She kissed me back.

'So're you,' I said.

Then she grabbed my left cheek.

'You've got a yummy butt, too, Robert.'

I was showered and dressed in under five minutes. I'd recently had my hair cut very short. Didn't even need a drier these days.

'You look good,' she said.

I kissed her again.

'I hope your friend is going to be all right. The priest.'

'I hope so, too.'

A priest in a motel with another priest, this one dead. All sorts of lurid possibilities came reluctantly to mind.

I gave her another kiss, this one as much for my sake as for hers, and left.

Fifteen minutes later, I turned into the parking area of the Palms Motel. It was the sort of place the tabloids love, the peeling paint and broken neon sign and cracked windows symbols of the peeling and broken and cracked souls who inhabited the rooms themselves. Whores got murdered here sometimes – usually forlorn black girls from the wrong end of the south-east side, or ample farm maidens from one of the small towns surrounding Cedar Rapids.

I found Room 154 and pulled into the closest available parking spot.

I lingered a moment in the cold morning rain, the hard relentless kind of spring downpour only the farmers love. I looked around to see if anybody was watching. Down at the far end of the sidewalk, a man in a white cowboy hat and a brown western suit came out of his room, carrying a thick briefcase. He rattled the door knob several times to make sure it was locked, then got into his big Chevrolet van.

When he was done backing up and turning around, headed in the opposite direction, I walked over to 154 and knocked.

Father Steven Gray opened the door immediately.

ii

The room was dark and tomb-cold. The only light came from the bathroom in the back. There was a mixture of smells: mildew, dirty rugs, towels, linen, and death. The dead man had shit himself. He lay hunched fetus-style in the middle of the double bed. He was without shirt or socks. His pants were unbuckled. I wasn't sure what to make of any of these details. His mouth was open as if in a silent scream, the lips violent red with blood.

I stood in the room and let myself be suffused with its history, all the betrayals and loneliness. The furnishings, stained, chipped, and dusty, looked too dirty to sit on.

'What's his name, Steve?'

'Father Daly. Peter Daly.'

'From St Mallory's?'

'Yes.'

I took a penlight from my sport jacket and knelt down next to the bed. I wanted a closer look at the wound in the chest. It was a large one. I suspected he'd been stabbed several times in the heart. But his open mouth was even more perplexing. This was not commonly seen in a murder victim. I shone my light inside and gagged. My entire body spasmed. I'd never seen anything like this.

'What is it?' Steve said.

'His tongue has been cut out.'

'Oh, my Lord.'

I went in the back and looked in the bathroom. Though I saw no blood I smelled some, probably in the dirt-and mustard-colored carpeting. The police lab man would use a test called Luminol to see if there was indeed blood in the rug.

Steve Gray followed me around like a child trailing a parent. He wore a white button-down shirt, a blue windbreaker, chinos and Reeboks. I wondered if the Pope ever dressed like that.

'You looking for anything in particular, Robert?'

'Not really,' I said.

When I came out of the bathroom, he said, 'We need to talk.'

I shook my head. 'Talk is for later. What we need to do now is call the police. You can't afford to stall them any longer.'

'I called two other people,' he said. 'And they're on their way over.'

'Who are they?'

'Bob Wilson, who is the President of the Parish Board, and Father Ryan. He's the only priest left at St Mallory's now – besides me, I mean.' He stared down at the dead priest. 'We don't always agree, Father Ryan and I, but this time we do.'

'Why invite them now?'

He raised his gaze from the corpse on the bed.

'They're better at press relations than I am. I'll need their help.'

I surveyed chairs, end-tables, bed and bathroom counters for anything that had been left behind. There was a golden earring on one of the end-tables. It had been cast in the shape of a heart. I left it where it was. The lab folks would be very angry if I didn't. An open condom wrapper on the bed proclaimed itself to be of the ribbed variety, with a 'special' tip.

'Is that what they call a French tickler?' Steve said.

'Uh-huh.'

18

He made a face. 'He was quite a guy.'

I didn't want to touch the phone so I walked out of the room and went up to the office. Steve walked alongside me.

'The night man here goes to St Mallory's,' he said. 'He'd had complaints about some kind of fight going on in the room. When he let himself in and found Father Daly dead, he called me right away.'

'What's the night man's name?'

'Paul Gaspard.'

'Let's go see him. I'm not sure he did you any favors. The cops're really going to be mad.'

'This will hurt the parish,' he said, not heeding me. 'The scandal. I can hear all the jokes already.'

We passed a series of junk cars lined up along the walk. They all had out-of-state plates – Missouri, Wisconsin, Minnesota . . . drifters drifting, desperately trying to find justice or at least shelter from injustice. They'd work minimum wage for a time, maybe enroll their two or three scruffy youngsters in a local school, and then some night they'd do something crazy, or something crazy would be done to them, and they'd start drifting again. You see the kids sometimes, peering out the back windows of rusty old cars. They can break your heart.

Just before we reached the office, I said, 'What was Father Daly doing here?'

'I don't know.'

I stopped and looked at him. With his pugged nose and curly dark hair, his face would always look younger than his years.

'You wouldn't lie to me, would you, Steve? I'm trying to help you, remember?'

He looked away from me. Big semis pushed into the sheets of rain marching down the nearby interstate. All the cars had their lights on, fragile prayers in a world of thunder and lightning and darkness.

He turned back to me. 'I think he was having an affair.'

'Who with?'

19

His smile was sour, his tone defensive. 'Despite what the tabloids have to say about us, most priests have affairs with women, not other men or little children.'

Steve hadn't given a name. I decided to ignore that for a while.

'Couldn't he get in trouble for having an affair?'

Steve nodded. 'Yes, and especially in this diocese. Bishop Curry doesn't put up with anybody breaking the vow of chastity. He has also been known to turn pedophile priests over to the police. He's a tough guy.'

'Was Father Daly a nice guy?'

He shrugged, glanced up at the line of raindrops dripping from the edge of the overhang that kept us dry. Everything smelled cold. Everything looked drab and sad.

'I'm not sure anybody would have called him nice.'

'He have any enemies?'

'A couple, as a matter of fact.'

'Any idea who they might be?'

'Well,' he said, 'for starters I'd say the husbands of the two women he had affairs with while he was supposed to be counseling them on their marriages. The husbands weren't at all happy about that. In fact, one of them was going to sue Father Daly for alienation of affection.' He smiled bleakly. 'I guess there are some things we can forgive as priests that we can't as men. Father Daly caused a lot of trouble in his time, I'm afraid.'

'I take it you'll tell the police this?'

'I won't have any choice, will I?'

We went inside. When Steve saw the woman behind the counter, he said, 'Oh, where's Paul?'

'Paul left,' she said. 'His shift ended twenty minutes ago.' She nodded to an ancient dusty wall clock. She was maybe sixty with dentures that clicked and an angry snarl of hair that a beautician had tinted an impossible orange. 'Help you gentlemen?'

'May I use the phone here?'

She pushed a black phone toward me. 'Long as it's local.'

'He's calling the police,' Steve said. 'There's a dead man in Room 154.'

'Oh Lord, not another one,' she said calmly.

'Another one?' I asked as I dialed.

'Couple years ago they found some hooker with her throat cut. There must've been cops here for two weeks, traipsing in and out. Scared the heck out of our customers. I mean, a lot of them don't want anybody to know they're here.'

I talked to a homicide detective and gave her all the information I had. She said that a black and white would be there within a matter of minutes, and that she herself would follow shortly afterwards.

Steve was over by the door. 'Father Ryan and Bob Wilson just pulled in. I'd better go back to the room.'

'I'll come with you,' I said. I pushed the phone back. 'Thanks.'

'You know the guy personally?' the woman asked me.

'Yes,' Steve said, and I could see the pain it caused him to say this. 'He was a priest.'

'You're kidding me,' the woman said. 'A priest!' Her dentures clicked and she made a grim face. 'Boy, you just don't know who to trust these days, do you?'

We walked back to Room 154.

Father Ryan was a tall, slender man with thinning blond hair and thick eyeglasses. He was dressed in priestly black, and a white Roman collar. He had a steel handshake.

Bob Wilson was big, beefy, whiskey-faced, and blustery. He had the air of a good bar-room brawler that his gray business suit, white shirt and blue tie couldn't quite offset. While he was still shaking my hand, he said to Steve Gray, 'This is great. We're supposed to start our fund-raising drive next week, Monsignor.'

'We'll be all right, Bob, just stay calm,' Steve said. I remembered him saying that Wilson and the priest would know how to handle the press. Given his air of frenzy, I wouldn't let Wilson anywhere near the press.

I went over to the door, pushed it open and marched

inside. They followed me. We were like teenagers at a carnival, about to gaze upon one of the world's most frightening sights: a murdered man.

'Boy, what did he do?' Bob Wilson said as soon as he was inside. 'Crap his pants or what?'

Father Ryan was more solemn. He went over and stood next to the bed and stared down at Father Daly's body.

He reached out a long arm and touched the dead priest's shoulder. Then he closed his eyes and began praying silently.

We all stood in silence until he was finished. I checked out the room with a couple of glances. Everything was as it had been – bathroom light on, door ajar, ashtrays clean, rusty metal wastebasket empty and tipped over on its side, golden earring on end-table, black oxfords and socks near the head of the bed, man's white shirt tossed over the back of a chair.

When he opened his eyes, Father Ryan said, 'I got to know his sister pretty well, Monsignor. She's over in Omaha. I can call her if you'd like.'

'I'd appreciate that, Father.'

Wilson, all angry energy, was stalking around the room.

'What was he doing here, anyway? Cheap motel like this. God Almighty.'

Yeah, he'd make a beautiful press spokesman all right.

He started to pick up the ashtray.

'Don't touch anything,' I said.

Wilson looked first at Steve and then at me. 'Exactly who are you, anyway, Mr Payne?'

'Robert was an FBI agent for a little over ten years,' Steve said. 'Now he's a consultant on murder cases to police departments.'

Wilson said, 'Oh. Sorry I snapped at you then. I guess you know what you're talking about after all.'

He walked back to the bathroom. 'All right if I pee? I've had three cups of coffee and no breakfast.'

'I wish you'd go down to the office, if you wouldn't mind,' I said. 'The police may find something useful in the toilet bowl.'

'What a job,' he said, 'pawing through toilet bowls.'

He left and Steve said, 'He's actually a very decent family man.'

Before I could say anything, Father Ryan said, 'He works very hard for our parish, Mr Payne. We wouldn't have been able to make any of the church improvements if it hadn't been for Bob Wilson.'

Steve was nodding agreement, when the two uniforms came through the door.

They introduced themselves and started the process of securing the crime scene.

'I'm afraid we'll have to ask you to wait outside,' the young uniform said. 'I understand that they have coffee and rolls down in the office.'

I was just turning to go when I glanced over at the end-table where the golden earring had been.

I walked across to the table and looked around at the floor, in case the earring had been knocked off.

But the earring was gone, even though I'd seen it just a few minutes ago.

I looked at Steve, Father Ryan, and Bob Wilson.

Only Bob Wilson had been anywhere near it. Only Bob Wilson could have taken it.

But why was an earring found at the crime scene so important to a good family man like him?

iii

'He's a friend of yours – Monsignor Gray?' Detective Judy Holloway asked me. Then: 'Excuse me.'

She sneezed then jammed the nipple of a small white plastic inhaler into her left nostril. 'You think I'm bad off,' she said, talking as if she had a cold. 'You should hear my three kids.'

Her sinuses quelled at least for the moment, she repeated, 'So is Monsignor Gray a friend of yours?'

'Uh-huh. Old friend.'

'You should sit him down and explain the law to him, then,' she said. She was a slender woman about five-eight. She wore a red blazer, starched white button-down shirt, black skirt, black hose and black one-inch pumps. She wasn't exactly pretty but there was an earnest quality to the blue eyes I liked. Her haircut was earnest, too – short and clean and sincere. She looked almost like a kid, no more than mid-thirties.

She'd spent twenty minutes in Room 154, then another ten minutes interviewing Steve Gray down in the office. I was outside the room, drinking coffee from a paper cup. A rusty garbage truck was consuming the contents of two dumpsters, the hydraulic arms making a lot of noise. A drizzle had started fifteen minutes ago and was still soaking everything down. A cop walked over in the rain and

25

jumped up on the garbage truck and told the guy to stop hauling the garbage away. The crime scene was being secured. The police team would want to look through the contents of the dumpster.

'I told him he should have called the police first,' I replied.

She said, 'You think he had anything to do with it?'

'With what?'

She sounded as if I were awfully naive. 'With what? Boy, Payne, you're supposed to be a pro. You find a man in a motel room with a dead man, who's your first suspect going to be?'

'You don't know Steve Gray.'

'No, I don't – but *you* do, and that's why I asked. I mean, they could have been gay.'

'Not Steve. And from what Steve said, not Father Daly, either.'

She nodded. 'Yeah, he told me that Daly had had a number of affairs. I don't know why these guys don't just become ministers. You see that French tickler wrapper in there?'

'Uh-huh.'

'He was one wild priest.'

'I'll be sure and mention that to the Pope next time I talk to him.'

'Smart-ass. Tim Brady says you're a good guy. I'll take his word for it.'

Brady is a Cedar Rapids detective I once worked with on a case in downtown Illinois. A kidnapping. Brady had been a young cop there.

'I think I irritated Father Gray's friend,' Detective Holloway said.

'Father Ryan?'

'No, the ball-player. I think he thought I wasn't reverent enough to the Monsignor.'

'Ball-player?'

'Yeah. Bob Wilson.'

'You got me. I'm not much of a sports fan.'

'All-American fullback when he was at Iowa. Played a couple of seasons in the pros then came back here and made a lot of money selling real estate. Owns his own company now and is doing very well.'

And one of his hobbies is collecting earrings, I thought.

I was just about to bring it up, how I suspected that Wilson had taken the earring, when a uniformed female cop approached Holloway and told her that the medical examiner wanted to see her in the room.

Holloway put out a hand. As we were shaking she said, 'Don't forget to tell your friend the Monsignor how the law works around here.'

'I won't.'

I was watching her walk away when somebody behind me said, 'He got a phone call late last night.'

I turned around to see Father Ryan there. He had a pink-frosted cake donut in one hand and a paper cup of coffee in the other.

'This probably doesn't look too good, does it?' he said.

'What doesn't?'

'You know, eating a donut at a time like this. Especially a pink one. I mean, with Father Daly in there dead.'

'You didn't like him much, huh?'

'You can tell?'

'Yeah. Sort of, anyway.'

'He was a bully, if you want to know the truth.'

'Steve Gray doesn't seem crazy about him, either.'

'He gave Steve – the Monsignor, I mean – a lot of trouble over the past couple of years. He pretty much flaunted his women.'

'How many women are we talking about?'

He sipped at his coffee. 'Excuse me. I want to get some of it down before it gets cold.'

'Sure.'

He finished sipping and said, 'Maybe six, seven. All of them women Father Daly was seeing as a counselor. Not to be cynical, but this is exactly the sort of thing the Catholic

27

Church gets sued over these days. It creates a lot of bad publicity. And we don't need any more.'

'You said something about a phone call.'

This time, I had to wait until he took a bite of his festive pink donut. He swallowed in two gulps that ran his Adam's apple up and down in a big lump.

'Last night,' he said, 'I was watching Leno in the den that Father Daly and I shared. Must've been about eleven o'clock. The phone rang. I got it on the second ring. But Father Daly was already talking. And there was a woman on the other end.'

'Did you recognize her voice?'

'Afraid not.'

'Did you hear anything she said?'

'Not really. I just hung up. I didn't want to butt into his business.'

'What time did you go to bed?'

'Maybe midnight.'

'Was Father Daly still home?'

'Yes. I heard him in his room as I passed it.'

'Any more phone calls?'

'None that I heard,' he said.

Steve Gray walked up, then. 'She gave me a good chewing out.'

'I kind've thought she might.'

'I should've called the police right away. It's just that we've got this fund-raising drive coming up and—'

'We're going to be fine,' Father Ryan said. 'People don't think that all priests have affairs.'

I wasn't sure about that. The Catholic Church had taken some tremendous hits in the past few years.

Wilson had disappeared for a time and now he was back.

'I don't like that detective,' he said. 'Arrogant bitch.'

'I thought she was very professional,' I said.

He looked at me and smiled. 'I don't think that you and I are ever in danger of becoming good friends, do you?'

'I'd agree there isn't much danger of that.'

He tapped his wrist-watch. 'I'm supposed to be at Rotary in another hour. Doing a big advance dog-and-pony show there over lunch. Father Ryan's helping me. We need to get moving.'

Everybody said goodbye. Steve and I walked back down to the office.

I went up to the desk clerk. 'All right if I see the register?'

'Fine by me.'

It sat on the desk. I turned it around so I could read the signatures.

'David Montrose' was the name Father Daly had used. He wrote it clearly on the fourth line. He was the only check-in the motel had had after 11:30 last night. Given the time-table Father Ryan had laid out for me, this had to be Daly.

'Thanks,' I said.

'Anything?' Steve said.

I put a dollar on the counter. We walked over to the Mr Coffee, took a couple of paper cups, and filled them.

'He used the name "David Montrose." That mean any-thing?'

'His brother-in-law's last name is Montrose. His brother's name is David.'

We walked back outside.

'Holloway thinks you may have had something to do with it,' I said.

'With the murder?'

'Uh-huh.'

'That's crazy.'

'That's what I told her.'

'Good Lord.'

'Don't get excited – it's how cops think. You're in a room with a dead man. The most logical suspect is you.'

'I suppose. But still.' His face was suddenly flushed, and he didn't say anything else.

The crime-scene search was still going on. We watched the next ten minutes of it. By now, most of the gawkers were gone.

The body came out in a plastic bag. The crime lab people brought out all their equipment. And Detective Holloway kept glancing back at Steve.

'She really does think I did it,' he said.

'Automatic reflex,' I said. 'I don't think you're a serious suspect.'

'I hope not,' he said. 'That's all the parish needs with this fund-raiser coming up. A dead priest and a Monsignor under suspicion.'

I went over and said goodbye to Holloway.

'He's nervous,' she said.

'Steve?'

'Yeah.'

'He's nervous because you keep looking at him.'

'Maybe he's nervous because he did it.'

'Maybe he's nervous because you're kind of an intimidating person.'

'I am?'

'Yeah. Kind of.'

She grinned. 'I'm going to take that as a compliment, Payne. I really am.'

Steve walked me over to my car.

'I've been thinking about it, Robert, and I want to hire you.'

'Hire me for what?'

'To find out what happened here.'

The wind was up again. Mist chilled my face.

'The police'll do a good job,' I said.

'I'd feel better if you were working on it, too, Robert. You were in the FBI.'

I smiled. 'So were a few other people, Steve. It's not like I was the only employee.'

'Please, Robert,' he said. 'The sooner this is resolved, the better for everybody.'

I checked my watch. 'I've got about three hours' work ahead of me right now, Steve. Why don't I stop over to the rectory after work today? We'll talk about it some more.'

'I really appreciate this, Robert.'

I tapped his shoulder. 'You're a good man, Steve. This'll all work out and not drag your fund-raising down at all. You'll see.'

'Thanks again,' he said.

Twenty minutes later, I was at the lawyer's offices.

iv

Six months after I joined the law firm of Doucette, Fineman & Cary, the largest criminal-law firm in the state of Iowa, I started thinking about writing a book. I even had the title: *Lawyers Are People, Too – More Or Less.*

Three things you need to know about Brad Doucette. He graduated number two in his class at Yale; he has won more 'impossible' cases than anybody in state history; and he once saw Madonna running naked down a Chicago hotel corridor.

I remember these things because Brad reminds me about them at least once a week.

Brad is a gadget guy. His outsized office, for instance, is equipped with all kinds of gadgets.

An electronic Rolodex sits on his desk. The heavy wine-red drapes on all three windows can be opened or closed with a toggle switch built into his desk. The leather armchairs are even equipped with little motors that tilt them up and down and back and forth. And the Egyptians thought they were on to something epic and immortal with the pyramids.

The gadgets are Brad's rewards. He spent a few years as a public defender because it was the politically correct thing to do. But then he was smart enough to team up with Cary, a former county attorney. Together, Doucette and Cary could honestly argue that they had seen the courtroom from every angle.

At first, they joined a prestigious firm with a long solid history. But the place couldn't survive all the giant egos within the walls. Criminal lawyers are only slightly less egotistical than Benito Mussolini.

So Doucette and Cary opened up their own place and took on junior partners who could handle domestic law and real-estate law and corporate law, so that if the criminal business ever went soft, the other departments could carry the firm. Tom Fineman oversees these departments.

Brad Doucette said, 'You hear the one about the priest and the rabbi and the Episcopalian minister?' Brad is five-seven, stocky, handsome in a dark and slightly crude way, and as in love with himself as any starlet. He wears expensive suits and tells you without shame how much each one cost. Today's number was a tweedy British-cut. He was probably going to ride to hounds later. At least in his mind.

'You told it to me yesterday.'

'Shit. How about the gal with three tits?'

'That one I got last week.'

'How about—'

'The gay electrician?' I said.

'You asshole,' he said. He was serious. His greatest pleasure was going to the office every morning and telling everybody his joke for the day. He needed a new supply. Some of them he'd told us three or four times each.

'I already told you about the gay electrician?'

'You already told me about the gay electrician. How come you never tell jokes about white Protestant males?'

'You go out with the wrong kind of broads, Payne. All that feminist bullshit.'

I was in the tiny office they'd given me as the firm's in-house investigator. I'd come straight here from the motel where Father Daly had been found dead.

Brad said, 'You get hold of that Beverly Wright woman?'

'She's coming in and talking it over.'

'I'm counting on you, babe.'

'I'll do what I can, "babe." '

He laughed. 'You hate that "babe" shit, don't you?'

'Uh-huh,' I said. 'A lot.'

'If I didn't worry that you might think I was a fag, Payne, I'd kiss you on the lips.'

'Thank you for sparing me.'

A minute-and-a-half later, I heard him wander through the door of Cary's office and start in on the woman with three breasts gag.

Brad Doucette was never going to be my kind of guy.

Around two that afternoon, the sun came out. I called Children's Hospital and talked to one of the nuns and said that I'd be picking Susan up in half an hour.

I liked talking to the nuns. They brought back good memories of my Catholic schooldays. The ones I'd known were all the best kind of religious people – selfless, charitable and willing to help in even the most extreme situations. The priests got the glory but, in many cases, the nuns did a lot of the work.

Sister Ellen stood on the front steps. She wore a blue business suit and a white blouse and oxfords. No habit. Sister Ellen was the one who'd called me when one of the local TV stations had run a piece about me and my bi-plane. She'd said that the hospital was caring for a very sweet little girl who had cerebral palsy. Her name was Susan and she was nine, and she had been totally transfixed by the TV story on the barnstormer. Would I consider taking her up in it?

I'd taken her up the last five Thursdays running. In between times, we'd also gone to a couple of movies, a miniature golf course, and out to one of the malls where a dance contest was being held. I suppose, at least in some ways, Susan was the kid my late wife Kathy and I had never had. She also gave me the freedom of being concerned about somebody other than myself. That's the nice thing you get from caring about somebody else – you're able to escape the prison of your own ego. At least for a time.

Sister walked her over to my car, helped her up inside, and

then waved goodbye. Susan wasn't always strong. Today she looked exhausted.

'You sure you're all right to go flying?' I said.

I observed her as we drove. She looked paler than I'd ever seen her. I got scared when I was around her. I knew how easily life could slip away.

I asked her again if she felt okay.

'I'm just a little tired is all, Robert. But please let's go up, all right?'

How could I say no?

'You been behaving yourself?'

She smiled. 'Uh-huh.'

'Haven't robbed any banks lately?'

She giggled. 'Not that I can remember.'

'Burned down any buildings?'

'Nope.'

'Well, you really *have* been staying out of trouble. I'm proud of you.'

'Is Felice going to be here today?'

'Not today, honey. Maybe next week.'

'How come?'

'Oh, she's just got other things to do.'

Felice was a big hit with Susan. She'd come out to the airport on three different afternoons. All three times, Felice ended up drinking a little too much in the evenings. Sometimes the unfairness of life got to her. You see a kid like Susan, it isn't real easy to comprehend how any kind of deity could do something like that. 'The terrible wisdom of God,' Graham Greene called it. And it is terrible indeed sometimes.

'There it is!' Susan said fifteen minutes later as we drove through the gates to the small airport.

I should tell you about the plane. My uncle was a barnstormer. With his bi-plane, he dusted crops, flew mail and put on numberless shows at county fairs. I grew up wanting to have a bi-plane of my own and now I did. It has huge wheels, two open cockpits, and a rebuilt engine that makes a deafening noise. You can put her down with complete ease and safety on just about any small grass field in the country.

'Do I get to wear the goggles today?'

'You sure do,' I said.

'And the helmet?'

'Absolutely.'

When I got her in the second seat of the bi-plane, she reached for her leather Snoopy helmet and her goggles. She'd already put on the heavy jacket Sister Ellen always made her bring along.

'Are we ready?' she shouted down from her seat.

'Just about, sweetheart.'

I spent a few minutes checking everything over – fuse, valves, engine controls, engine and flight instruments. I even checked out the struts on the double wings. The bi-plane was built in 1929, an ancient venerable flying machine with mustard-colored sides. The wing panels are made of cloth and wood. This is about as close to a real bird as a flying machine will ever get.

I got her going with just one jerk on the propeller. Then I climbed in my cockpit.

'Here we go!' I said.

Susan's exultant laugh was silver music.

We flew for forty-five minutes. Below us, farmers did their early-season plowing and rivers were alive with a variety of boats. It was spring, or soon would be anyway, and it made everybody a little crazy. I swept low over one farm and the wife stood next to the silo and waved at me as if I were the Beatles about to land.

Susan especially liked tracking the limestone cliffs, so we spent at least half the time coming in low over the ragged jutting rocks above the river. She'd told me once about the early Indians who'd lived in limestone caves and how they'd been vegetarians and not meat-eaters at all.

When we were driving back to the hospital, Susan said,

'Have you ever had something you dreamed about come true?'

'Hmm,' I said. 'I guess I'd have to think about that. I'm not sure. Have *you* ever had something you dreamed come true?'

'Sister Ellen says maybe it's going to happen. She said that God does that sometimes, puts dreams in your head and has them come true.'

'So what dream're you having?'

'That I won't be sick any more.'

I was glad she couldn't see the tears in my eyes. 'Maybe it will come true, honey,' I said. 'Maybe it will come true.'

When I got her back to the hospital, she leaned over and gave me a quick kiss on the cheek.

'You think we could do this next week, Robert?' She asked this every week.

'I don't see why not.'

'Ooo goodie, I'll tell Sister Ellen.' Then, 'I really had fun today. Thank you, Robert.'

This was the formal part of the afternoon, the part that came directly from Sister Ellen straight through the mouth of nine-year-old Susan. Good manners.

'You're most welcome, my dear,' I said in my best Dracula voice.

She giggled. She loved the Dracula voice.

I delivered her unto Sister Ellen, who said, 'Did she tell you about her dream?'

'She certainly did.'

'You be sure and say a couple of prayers for her, Robert.'

'You bet I will.'

And I would, too. I prayed all the time. I just hoped there was somebody listening.

But I guess we all hope that, don't we?

I gave Susan a little more of Dracula and another kiss on the forehead, and then I was back in my car.

V

The rectory was built of the same soaring native stone as the church itself. It was also built in the days when great vaulting spires were mandatory. St Mallory's had been here for more than a hundred years now, the neighborhood changing from Czech to Irish to its present mix of black and Hispanic. Because of its south-east side location, it was the church of wealthy Catholics for the past seventy years. Even today, parked near garages defiled with graffiti and old black men who sat patiently on crumbling back porches waiting for their dreams to come true – even today you found Cadillacs and BMWs and Mercedes Benzes here.

Five generations of Irish Catholics had trooped through this venerable rectory, and sometimes it was fun to imagine them standing on the front steps, talking to the priests, the women of the last century in their bustles, the men of the early 1900s in their straw boaters, the men and women of WWII in their uniforms, and the hippie parents in tie-dyes and beards.

Right now, there were vans from two of the local TV stations parked at the curb, and the rain was back.

A woman of about sixty opened the rectory door to me. She wore a Lycra jogging suit and a buff blue headband that complemented the deeper blue of her suit. She had an angular face and white hair, but she exuded enough energy to charge up a generator. She was one of those wily, wiry older women who could probably put away a couple of boxers.

'Hello. I'm Robert Payne,' I told her. 'I'm here to see the Monsignor.'

'You're not a reporter, are you?' she asked.

I smiled. 'I haven't sunk that low yet.'

She smiled back. 'Careful, they might hear you. They're everywhere. I'm Bernice Clancy. Come on in. They're interviewing the Monsignor in his study,' Bernice said, leading me to the back of the place. 'Bob Wilson is with him.'

The rectory was old but impressive, with heavy drapes and carpeting, woodwork and wainscoting that would cost thousands of dollars today. The furnishings ran to formidable leather couches and chairs. The framed paintings were the biggest surprise, for they consisted of very nice prints of Van Gogh, Chagall and Picasso. Except for the paintings, the rectory recalled a gentler time – old Irish priests spending their nights in armchairs with pipe and slippers and western novels.

I followed Bernice down the narrow hallway that smelled of floor wax. We ended up in a large kitchen with a small breakfast nook in the corner. A slight and very pretty girl in a white sweater, jeans and sandals was dumping spaghetti into a colander.

'Will he be eating with us?' she asked. 'There's plenty.'

'Jenny, this is Robert Payne. He's a friend of the Monsignor's. Jenny's one of our housekeepers.'

She walked over to me, wiping water from her right hand on the leg of her stonewashed jeans.

She had a hard little hand. She also had freckles and about the most seductive blue eyes I'd ever seen. I'd taken her for maybe late teens but up close I could see a few streaks of gray in the dark hair she had cinched back in a pony tail.

'You're the FBI man the Monsignor mentioned this morning,' she said.

'Former FBI man, I'm afraid,' I said.

40

'Well, we're all "formerly" something, aren't we? I'm formerly a topless dancer.'

Her gaze was impish as she said this. She watched Bernice's reaction. I sensed some tension between them.

Jenny went over and slipped her arm through Bernice's. 'I like to shock her sometimes. She's so cute when she blushes.'

There was a lot of real affection in her voice, but it was not an affection shared by Bernice. She remained embarrassed, stiff and immobile.

'I like her, but she doesn't like me.'

'I just don't see why you have to keep dredging up the past is all, Jenny,' Bernice said. 'I don't believe in washing your dirty laundry in public.'

Jenny nodded and said to me, 'Seven years ago, one of the priests here got a high-school girl pregnant. With the publicity and all, a lot of parents took their kids out of school. Monsignor Gray and Bernice are always worried there'll be some new scandal.'

I said, 'I'm sure the situation with Father Daly isn't going to help. By the way, I'd like to talk to Father Ryan, too, if I could.'

Bernice smiled. 'You'll find him in his favorite place.'

'Oh?'

'The bell-tower. Here, I'll show you.'

Jenny put out her hand again and we shook. 'I hope I'll see you again, Mr Payne.'

'Me, too.'

Her hand lingered longer than it needed to and this was not lost on Bernice. She looked at our hands and then her gaze rose to rest, disapprovingly, on Jenny's face.

In the hall, Bernice said, 'She's too fresh.'

'Jenny?'

'Yes. In my day, young women knew their place, especially around priests. But not her. She flirts with them.'

'With Father Daly?'

'Yes. And with Monsignor Gray.'

We walked to a side door and then out to the sidewalk

41

between the rectory and church.

She paused. 'You know, there's something that's been bothering me since Father Daly died. As you're a former FBI man and all, maybe I should tell you about it.'

'Tell me what?'

'The night before he died, Father Daly called me at home. He said that he had something he wanted me to have.'

'He didn't say what?'

She looked at me and frowned. 'No – no, he didn't. And now that I think about it, it's kind of mysterious, isn't it?'

'Yes,' I said. 'It is.'

The church was empty, the altar dark, our footsteps echoing off the vaulted ceiling.

She led me to the back of the church, past the Stations of the Cross, past the confessional to a door beneath the bottom of the choir-loft.

'This is Father Ryan's favorite place,' Bernice said.

'This?' I said, puzzled. All I could see was the door.

'The bell-tower.'

She opened the door. I saw wooden stairs that climbed steeply and curved abruptly.

'After you,' I said.

We climbed.

I remembered how high the bell-tower appeared from the outside. It seemed even taller from the inside.

The staircase was narrow and dusty.

'You pooped yet?' Bernice said.

'Just about,' I said. My breath was coming harder, no doubt about it. The stairs seemed ever steeper, the dusty concrete walls ever narrower.

By the time we reached the bell-tower, a fine sweat had broken out on my back and arms, and my breath was coming in tiny gasps.

There was a square hole cut in the floor of the bell-tower. This was where the stairs ended.

'Mr Payne would like to talk to you, Father,' Bernice said

when we were all standing in the tower.

The tower gave the feeling of being wide open to the sky. There were large square cut-outs in each of the tower walls. If a person got careless, he could easily fall to his death.

'Nothing to be afraid of, Mr Payne,' Father Ryan said. Apparently he could sense my discomfort.

Bernice said, 'You haven't given him the speech, Father.'

Father Ryan smiled. 'Bernice is of the belief that I am overly attached to this bell and this tower.' He put a hand out and touched the huge bell. 'This is a special bell brought from Ireland sixty years ago. Do you know anything about bells, Mr Payne?'

'Afraid not, Father.'

Bernice was right. There was a pride and passion on the priest's face that hadn't been there before.

'This is real bell metal, Mr Payne,' Father Ryan said. 'A mixture of copper and tin – thirteen parts copper to four parts of tin. Bells of this type date all the way back to early Christianity. The Chinese used bronze for their bells. The Early Christians couldn't afford bronze, but ironically the copper and tin produced a better sound.'

'And you ring it by pulling the rope?' I said.

He nodded. 'The rope is attached to the metal clapper – and when the clapper strikes the bell, the ringing sound is produced.'

He walked over to one of the large open areas and pointed to the city below. 'On a beautiful day, this is like an eyrie up here, Mr Payne. It makes me feel a little bit like God.' He smiled subtly at me. 'You can admire humanity from afar – and sometimes that's the best way.'

While he spoke, I looked straight down to the darkness below. You could easily fall between the bell and the floor. And if you did fall, you'd never survive.

Then he said, 'I take it you came to see me about Father Daly, Mr Payne.'

'Yes,' I said. 'I wondered if you could show me his room in the rectory?'

'His room?'

'The Monsignor's busy so I thought I'd ask you. I'll probably have some questions for you, too.'

He looked out at the sky again. Even with the overcast and mist, it did feel like an eyrie up here – safe from all the grief and sorrows of the human soul.

'He didn't care about his room,' Father Ryan said.

'Oh?'

'Just dumped stuff here on the way in and out of the rectory.'

'He was a counselor, you said.'

'Right.'

'Where was his office?'

'Over in the school behind the church.'

'Why the school?'

'He said he wanted to be comfortable. Personally, I think the Monsignor intimidated him.'

'Oh? In what way?'

'You know, sort of like having your parents home when you had your girlfriend with you.'

The rose-colored wallpaper and the brass bed and the heavy mahogany bureau gave the room the feel of a hotel room of fifty years ago. On Father Daly's night-stand were paperbacks by Freud, Sartre, Martin Buber, and Proust.

'He read much fiction?'

'That was his dream,' Father Ryan said. 'To be a writer. He was real hung up on Proust and Sartre.'

'No popular fiction?'

'He hated popular fiction. He was something of a snob, in fact.'

He picked up a stack of CDs next to a small CD-player. 'All classical music.'

I watched him a long moment. 'I'm trying to figure out if you liked him.'

'Not much.'

'Why?'

'I told you he was a bully, and he was. He didn't think so, of course.' He smiled, and suddenly looked much younger. 'He just thought he was a member of a superior species. I always thought he should've been a Jesuit. He didn't like being a parish priest much. I saw him in a sick room once and he was pretty callous. He looked irritated that the wife of the dying man was crying so much.'

Even with the table-lamp on, the faded wallpaper and the somber woodwork made the room much darker than it should have been.

I was going through the bottom of the bureau when I found the newspaper clippings.

They'd been cut cleanly from the *Cedar Rapids Gazette* – two stories from last year detailing two different murders. The first was the murder of Tawanna Jackson, a thirty-one-year-old black woman, and the second, the murder of Ronald Swanson, a fifty-six-year-old white man.

'Was Father Daly a true-crime buff?'

'Not that I know of.'

'Can you make any sense of these?'

I handed the clippings over to him. While he scanned them, I opened the closet and peered inside. The stench of mothballs was overpowering. I've always imagined that if Time itself had a smell, it would be that of attics and mothballs.

Father Daly owned two black priestly suits, some sweaters, slacks, shirts, and three pairs of black boots.

'I don't know why he'd have these,' Father Ryan said, handing the clippings back to me. 'The only connection is they went to Mass here.'

'So why would Father Daly keep them?'

'The Monsignor always says the same thing when you ask him questions like that, Mr Payne,' he answered somberly.

'Oh?'

'He always says, "Now how would I know?" '

I laughed. 'Probably learned that in seminary.'

'Probably.'

I glanced at the clippings. 'You think he actually knew these people?'

'Probably. A priest gets to know most people in his parish.'

'You think he was seeing either of them as a counselor?'

He smiled. 'You really *are* a detective, aren't you, Mr Payne?'

'I sure try hard to be.'

He shrugged. 'I suppose I could find out. Whether he saw them in counseling, I mean.'

'Would you? I'd be very grateful for that.'

'You want to go downstairs and see how the Monsignor is doing?'

'Sure,' I said. 'I guess we're through up here.'

I handed him the clippings. 'Could I ask you to Xerox these? Then we'll put the originals back for the police.'

'I'll meet you downstairs in the den,' Father Ryan said. 'I'll run these copies first.'

'I'd appreciate it.'

He stared at the clippings. 'It is pretty strange he'd keep these, isn't it?'

'Yes,' I said. 'It is.'

Father Ryan switched off the table-lamp as we left the room.

Twenty minutes later he told me that neither Jackson nor Swanson had been in counseling.

vi

She was standing outside Steve Gray's den – a tall blonde woman with an elegant face and an even more elegant sorrow in her eyes. She wore a long draped black skirt, a gray tweed jacket and a frilly white blouse. She made me think of eastern girls' schools – that sort of aloof mysterious quality that doting prairie boys always attribute to upper-class girls. But the dark eyes, the grief of the dark eyes, made her doubly intriguing.

'Ellie Wilson, this is Robert Payne,' Father Ryan said.

We shook hands, her right arm encumbered by a tiny black leather purse tucked beneath it.

'You met Ellie's husband, Bob, this morning at the hotel.'

I didn't want to believe it. The romantic in me cried foul. How could a woman like this settle for a beefy manipulator like Bob Wilson?

I looked into the study. Seated behind a table in the large room were Steve Gray and Bob Wilson. They were encircled by portable TV lights. Four stations had microphones set up on the table.

I spent a few minutes watching the action.

'What would a priest be doing in a hotel room, Monsignor?'

'Did you know that Father Daly had a secret life?'

'Did Father Daly ever get into any trouble before?'

'Had any parishioners ever complained about Father Daly?'

47

And so on.

If Bob Wilson was a master of manipulating the press, he wasn't having a good day.

He writhed, he scowled, he fumed, he stammered, he stumbled.

Finally, he said, 'I think we've been very fair to you folks. But this is about all the time we've got for interviews today.'

They started grumbling, the reporters, and then he cupped his hand over the closest microphone and said, 'I'd like to ask you all a favor. St Mallory's is starting its fund-drive next week. If you know anything about the state of church finances today, you'll know that we really need to reach our goal. And it's not going to help us if you play up the sleazy side of all this.'

A few of the reporters smiled.

A priest found half-naked and dead in a motel room is going to come out sleazy no matter how carefully you report it.

A couple reporters tried more questions but neither Steve nor Wilson were having any. They stood up and walked out of the study. The journalists and camera people stayed behind and started packing up their equipment.

'Hi, Robert,' Steve Gray said when he saw me.

Bob Wilson frowned. Then he went over and possessively slid his arm around his wife and gave her a small peck on the cheek.

'I don't know about anybody else, but I could use a drink,' Steve said. 'Anybody care to join me?'

'I'm afraid I've got a terrible headache,' Ellie Wilson said. She gave her husband's arm a squeeze. 'My car's here. I'll just drive myself home.'

'You sure?' Wilson said.

'You know how my headaches go,' she said.

'How about you, Robert?'

'Sure. I could go for a drink.'

'Good,' Steve said. 'There's a small study straight down the hall. Why don't we all just go in there?'

'I'll see you at home later,' Ellie Wilson said, kissing her husband on the cheek.

Thunder rumbled down the sky. She flinched a little, Ellie Wilson, and looked exceedingly distraught. Most adults didn't get that upset by thunder.

'Good night, Monsignor,' she said, reaching across to touch Steve's arm.

That was when her small black leather purse that had been tucked into her arm fell to the floor.

It popped open on impact, its contents spilling directly in front of my shoes.

Most of the items were about what you'd expect: gum, mascara, hand mirror, nail file, car keys.

The one item I didn't expect to see was the heart-shaped earring I'd noticed in Father Daly's motel room. Or its duplicate.

I bent over and pushed the things back into her purse. Except for the earring.

When I stood up and handed her the purse, I held the earring between my thumb and forefinger.

She was looking at it greedily, as if she wanted to snatch it from my fingers.

Her husband Bob wore another expression. He looked as if he wanted to smash my face in.

'That's a very nice earring, Mrs Wilson,' I said. 'I take it you have the mate.'

Wilson himself ended up snatching it from my fingers.

He took it brusquely, dropped it in the open purse she held in her hands, and then clamped it shut.

'There you go,' he said. 'I'll see you at home a little later.'

Beautiful Ellie Wilson said goodnight to each of us and then left, elegant, cool, sorrowful. She held on to her purse very tightly now.

2:

POLICE DEPARTMENT

Lawrence Michael Lynnward
Age: 23
Race: Caucasian
Occupation: Unemployed
Marital Status: Single
Military Service: None

Lynnward: My dad says at least they used to sneak
around about it. He said a nigger ever
walked into a bar with a white gal
around here; he'd get the shit kicked out
of him. Not today. They're brazen about
it. You see 'em walkin' down the street
in broad daylight, their black arm
around their white girls. My dad says
it's the Jews who brought this on. He
says it was the Jews who gave the
niggers the idea that they were equal to
white people. The coons want white
girls . . . fine. My dad says when he was
a little boy back in Mississippi he saw
the Klan hang this Jew newspaper
editor once . . . he said it was real
beautiful, the way the fire looked on the
white robes and the big burning cross
right in front of the Jew when he was

hangin' there dead . . . All my dad says about me burnin' down that synagogue is, you just be careful. They got them god-damned federals workin' undercover everywhere these days. But I'm smart . . . I drive to a town where nobody knows me . . . and find me a synagogue. Used to be I did black churches and maybe I will again someday. But right now I'm just gonna keep on concentratin' on the Jews.

Lawrence Lynnward

Pop always makes it their little private joke. Mom'll put the dinner on the table and Pop'll look across at Larry and say, 'Guess the boy'n me'll do some huntin' tonight.'

'Huntin'?' Mom'll say. 'What're you huntin' this time of year?'

Pop grins. 'Oh, you'd be surprised what we can find.'

Then he winks at Larry and twelve-year-old Larry winks back.

. . . Awhile later Larry and Pop're in the pick-up truck and driving into Cedar Rapids from the acreage where they live.

Pop's got his .45 on the seat right next to his whiskey flask. Larry can tell, the way he's hunched over the wheel and really giving the Chevy some gas, that Pop's excited. Real excited.

And so is Larry. But he's scared, too. What if he can't do it?

'How you feelin'?' Pop says, looking over at him and grinning. 'You think you can handle it tonight?'

Last time, couple weeks ago, Larry didn't handle it so good. Bastard got away.

'I think I'm ready, Pop.'

'You practice every afternoon like I said?'

'I sure did.'

'You try them knots the way I showed you?'

'Yes, sir I did.'

'Then there shouldn't be no problem, should there, Larry?'

55

'No, sir. I don't guess so.'

Wants to pee his pants, he's so scared now, the way Pop's talking to him and everything.

What if he can't do it? He doesn't know if he can take another beating the way he did a couple of weeks ago. Mom had to look at his privates and she said they were all black and blue from Pop's belt, Pop being the sort who gets you real good back *and* front.

. . .and anyway he wants to do it for himself, doesn't want to fail again, seems like he's always failin' somethin' or other, school or sports or just hangin' out with the other kids, who don't really like him because he's so small for his age and he always wears them bib overalls Mom always buys . . .

. . . doesn't want to fail, no sir . . . and won't fail tonight, no sir he won't . . .

They cruise on into the city, which Larry likes. He likes the city darkness and the neon and the shiny cars and the tall buildings and the pretty ladies on the street. He daydreams about their breasts, knowing they look like the ladies in the dirty magazines Pop hides from Mom in the basement. And he likes the hot cars the teenagers drive up and down First Avenue, their radios thundering, their windows rolled down so they can yell 'Hey pussy! I got somethin' for ya!' and stuff like that to the beautiful high school girls at the Dairy Queen and the A&W Root Beer stand and 7-11. Someday he'll live here, has wanted to live here since he was a little kid . . .

Pop takes a sudden right turn, the old pick-up rattling as he does so, and almost immediately Larry can smell the river. No smell like it on a July night. Heat and fish and dirty water, an oddly sweet-sour scent that is unlike anything he's smelled before.

'You ready for a little coon huntin'?' Pop says, which is what he always says. And grins.

Larry grins back. 'Yeah, I sure am, Pop.'

He reaches down into the darkness and finds the rope.

'You tie that knot the way I told ya to?'

'I sure did, Pop.'

Pop grins. 'Good boy.'

They're on dark side streets now so Pop decides to have himself a little swig from the flask.

The houses in this area are small and shabby. Coon town, as Pop always calls it. Where the niggers live.

Pop isn't crazy enough to go into the heart of it. He goes around it. There's a half block of taverns and a sandy road leading to a small section of trailers. This is on the outskirts of the area. White man'd have to be a crazy sumbitch to go in there at night.

'Get it ready.'

'It's ready, Pop.'

They're abreast of the taverns now. Young blacks, about half with dread locks and half with shaved heads, stare sullenly at the pick-up truck as it floats by. Gangsta rap music snarls in the night. The cars parked along the streets all have decorations all over them, mud flaps and white fuzzy stuff on the steering wheels and all kinds of lights that blink on and off. Pop says you give a colored man a brand new Caddy, he'll have it junked up within twenty-four hours.

Larry's mouth is dry now. He sure doesn't want to miss tonight. He sure doesn't.

They leave the block of taverns and turn up toward the small park that sits way up high on the hill above the river.

Larry and his Pop always work different areas of the city. They haven't been over here in some time. Last time they came to the city in fact they weren't coon hunting at all. They spray-painted a swastika on the front door of a synagogue.

The thing is to find one alone. Around here, so close to their own kind and all, they feel safe. They're always walking around just the way white people do.

They spot one.

Kid. Not much older than Larry. Walking down from the darkened pavilion up there. Wearing Levi cut-offs and a sleeveless white T-shirt. So black he's almost invisible when he's out of the street light's range.

This is actually kind of nice up here. Five, six degrees

cooler, for one thing. For another, you can smell flowers and hear crickets. Kinda peaceful, actually.

'Ready?' Pop says.

'Ready.'

The thing is to swoop up fast like, before the kid even has time to offer the least resistance.

He's walking on the right side of the road, perfect for Larry to lean out and do his job.

'Here he comes,' Pop says, as they swoop up right next to the kid.

Larry half-jumps out of the window – the truck is still moving, though at around ten miles per hour – and throws the lasso around the kid's shoulders, just the way cowboys rope a steer.

Perfect!

The kid screams.

They'll have to act fast or half the coons in Cedar Rapids'll be up here.

Drag him fast up the street, that's the thing they have to do.

The kid, who is a lot stronger than he looks, puts up a pretty good fight until Pop really floors it . . . and then the kid doesn't have a chance.

He's jerked off his feet and flung to the ground.

And then Pop starts dragging him, already hitting forty miles an hour.

The kid is screaming and wailing and cussing as he's tugged along in the wake of the truck, his skin already suffering terrible friction burns, and his head slamming against the asphalt.

Larry holds tight on the rope. He got the first part down perfect – throwing the rope and lassoing the coon real good – now he can't let down and let the rope slip out of his hands.

At first, even though he's being pulled along, the kid fights back so Larry needs all his strength to keep hold of the rope.

But after a few hundred yards . . . Larry can feel the coon losing his strength.

The kid is still screaming and now in the darkness they can

hear other colored voices shouting in fear and panic, wondering what's happening in their neighborhood.

'Cut the rope!' Pop says.

Larry's been holding his switchblade in his right hand.

Now that Pop's given him the signal, Larry moves fast, snicking the blade open, and slashing through the rope.

Moments later, Larry is smiling to himself and pulling the slit rope inside the truck.

There won't be no beating tonight. No, sir. He did it just right.

Pop is all concentration now, highballing it out of the black section of town, out north to where the river winds in the wind and moonlight, the shores all shaggy with pines, Pop says, 'Undo that flash for me!'

'Yes, sir.'

'You want a drink?'

'Really?'

'You done a man's work, you should get a man's pay.'

'Great!' Larry feels like he's eighteen years old or something.

'Just don't tell your Mom, you hear me?'

'Oh, I hear you, Pop,' Larry says, this big shit-eatin' grin splittin' his face, 'I hear ya real good.'

Larry can't ever remember being this happy, not even the time he found the five dollar bill in the parking lot of the baseball stadium.

Not even then.

They showed the coons, boy, they showed them real, real good.

Two

i

The bar was over on the west side, near an industrial park. You didn't need to go inside to hear the country western jukebox, and you didn't need to be a sleuth to know that this was a place where ordinary middle-class people like me should fear to tread.

There were maybe thirty motorcycles parked in front of the Death's Head Tavern. The skull and bones on the sign above the door matched the skull and bones on the T-shirts of the men and women inside.

It was sort of like a western movie. As soon as I walked inside, everybody stopped talking and turned to glower at me. The women were just as scary as the men. If you counted up all the tattoos in this place, the number would probably reach the 1,500 mark. To say nothing of scars, broken noses, glass eyes and artificial limbs. Born to be wild.

The bar was darker than night, with the only real light coming from the illuminated tiers of bottles behind the bar, the revolving Bud clock above the bar, the jukebox and a lone bulb over the pool-table.

A guy who looked like Captain Hook on steroids said, 'I'd say you were in the wrong place, dude.'

His buddies all laughed so hard their tattoos jiggled on their biceps. So did all the knives and chains they wore warrior-style on their bodies.

'You hear what I said?' Captain Hook asked when I didn't turn around and run away.

'I'm supposed to meet somebody here,' I said.

There was an open slot along the bar so I filled it. The bartender looked pretty much like his clientèle. Long, scraggly hair, sleeveless black T-shirt, and a face that was almost ludicrously mean.

'You just don't dig, do you, man?' the bartender said. 'I ain't gonna serve you. Now get your ass out of here.'

'I'll have a beer,' I said. 'Draft beer. Bud.'

I knew I was yammering. I was scared. And I was pissed. Gilhooley had apparently set me up for some kind of practical joke.

I first met Gilhooley one long-ago morning in ROTC at the University of Iowa. This was back when ROTC was still mandatory, though the entire program would be scrapped a year later.

Gilhooley was the only ROTC cadet dressed in full blue uniform with a copy of *Marxist Dialectic* in his hand.

He hasn't changed much. To him, the sweetest days in memory will always be those times when the streets of Iowa City were packed with angry student demonstrators. The night the ROTC building was burned to the ground is the most hallowed of all evenings.

I like to remind Gilhooley as often as possible that I'm a registered Republican.

These days, Gilhooley edits an Iowa historical magazine, and does research for a number of law firms and investigative agencies. Gilhooley can give you all sorts of information nobody else can seem to find.

He's especially good at background checks. That's why I was meeting him – to give him some work. But he'd apparently decided he wanted to pull one of his practical jokes by sending me into a hell-hole like this one.

Captain Hook grabbed me, spun me around and was just pulling his arm back, ready to shatter my face with his fist, when I heard a toilet flush and then heard a squeaky-hinged door open up.

'Kill the sumbitch,' one of Hook's buddies said.

'Break his face,' said one of the ladies' auxiliary.

'Make him a soprano,' said one guy over by the jukebox.

I was trying to figure out the best way to remove myself from Captain Hook's grasp when a familiar voice said, 'Hey, Payne, I see you met my buddies here.'

'You know this creep?' Captain Hook demanded when Gilhooley appeared in the light from the Bud clock.

'Sure I know him. He's all right.'

'He looks like a narc,' Captain Hook said.

'Nah,' Gilhooley said. 'He used to be a fed but now he's private. I told him to meet me here.'

Captain Hook glowered at me a little more then let go of my shirt.

'Hey, c'mon now, let's everybody have a beer,' Gilhooley said. 'And my buddy Payne here will buy it.'

A kind of cheer went up, the jukebox kicked on, and the bartender started setting up cans of beer along the bar. Free beer. Unless your name was Payne.

'Hey,' Gilhooley said to me. 'I want you to meet my friends, Robert.'

There was a semi-circle of them fanned out around us. Captain Hook said, 'Gilhooley here's been tellin' us all about Chairman Mao and shit like that.'

'Chairman Mao was one cool dude,' said one of the other bikers.

'Power to the people, man,' said another.

'Fucking capitalist pigs, man,' said yet another.

Somehow, Gilhooley had managed to turn all these bikers into Maoists. It was just like living in Iowa City in 1968. Gilhooley had found heaven.

'Hey, Robert, I want you to meet my friends,' he said again.

Four or five guys stuck their hands out. Now that they knew I was with Chairman Gilhooley, their opinion of me had changed.

'Robert, this is Pig Face, this is Gravel Pit, this is Long

Dong, this is Knuckle Duster, and this is Snake Lips.'

'Hey,' they all said.

'Hey right back,' I said.

'These guys are committed,' Gilhooley said. 'Not like those candy-asses we went to college with. These guys will never sell out, will you, Pig Face?'

'Right on,' said Gravel Pit.

'Right *fucking* on,' said Long Dong.

I led Gilhooley down to the end of the bar so we could talk alone.

'You idiot,' I said.

'Idiot? What're you talking about, man?'

'Bringing me into a dump like this.'

'Dump? These guys are real revolutionaries, Robert. Mao-ists.'

'Right.'

'They are, man.'

'If they're such revolutionaries, ask them what they think about black people or feminists or gays.'

'I'm bringing them along real slow,' Gilhooley said. 'We'll get to all that stuff later.'

'Right. For the time being you'll just concentrate on the fun stuff, huh? Burning down buildings and shooting capitalists? I haven't heard that many people say "Right on" since the last time Jim Morrison exposed himself on stage.'

I forced myself to take a few deep breaths. To chill out, as Gilhooley called it.

I looked across at him and shook my head. I'd spent twenty years trying to hate him and I couldn't. Not quite. Buried in all the rhetoric and melodrama was a decent guy, one who genuinely cared about people less fortunate than himself. Unfortunately, he saw the cure for all our problems only in *isms*, most notably any *ism* that had as its sworn enemy the United States.

One other thing about Gilhooley: for a somewhat gangly, red-topped forty-three year old, he sure spends a lot of time with a lot of women. Maybe my generation of men has blanded out now that we're middle-aged. Or maybe certain women just like Gilhooley's passion, misplaced as it frequently is. Whatever the reason, Gilhooley sees more than his share of females.

'So what's the job?' he said.

I told him about the murder. And about the people involved. The Wilsons. Steve Gray. Father Ryan.

'A hurry on this?'

'As much as possible.'

'I should be able to get to it pretty fast.'

'I'd really appreciate it.'

'That's pretty strange, that priest dying in a motel room.'

'Yes, it is strange. They're just starting a fund-drive. This didn't come as real good news.'

'At least it gets them a little publicity.'

'You always find the bright spot, don't you?'

'Huh?'

'Never mind, Gilhooley. I'll talk to you tomorrow.'

Felice made us a dinner of vegetarian burgers and green beans. We alternated nights making meals.

Afterward, I went into the spare bedroom I use as my den and sat down at the table to study the copy of the clippings we'd found in Father Daly's room. I turned on the computer.

Then I laid the Xerox of the two newspaper clippings out in front of me and read them as I ate.

WOMAN SLAIN IN BOWKER PARK

Cedar Rapids Police identified the woman found stabbed to death in Bowker Park Tuesday night as Tawanna Jackson. Her eyes had been cut out.

Friends are baffled as to what Jackson was doing in the park, adding to the speculation that she was killed elsewhere and dropped in the park.

The clipping went on to say that close friends of Jackson's

had said that she had been acting 'stressed out' lately, though none offered an explanation of why.

MAN'S BODY FOUND IN CAR

Police Chief Michael Conroy held a press conference Thursday afternoon to confirm the name of the homicide victim discovered the night before. He had been stabbed to death, and his left ear had been cut off.

Conroy said that Ronald Swanson, 56, of Cedar Rapids, was found in the front seat of his car where it was parked behind the Lariat Lounge on A Ave N.W.

Tavern patrons said that Swanson had spent three hours in the tavern and had been drinking heavily.

The story concluded by noting that Swanson was an insurance company executive and a father of three. Services were pending.

Interesting.

Tawanna Jackson's eyes had been cut out. Ronald Swanson's ear had been cut off. And Father Daly's tongue had been cut out. There had to be a connection here.

The FBI taught me to analyze crimes, to do psychological profiles on criminals from what they did and didn't do, from what they left behind and what they took with them. Now, automatically, whenever I hear of a crime I start analyzing on the basis of what I know: what kind of person would have done this?

Why?

When a murdered man's possessions included news stories about two other murdered people, there ought to be a connection. There was something nagging my brain but staying just out of reach. And I wasn't surprised. Count up the sleep I'd had in the last two days and it didn't add up to much. It was time to rest, let the back of my mind work on those niggling things and bring them to the surface.

The phone rang just as I was carrying the dishes over to the sink.

My classically-striped cat Tasha was on the couch waiting for me to join her for a few hours of TV watching. Crystal and Tess, the other two cats, were lying side by side in the armchair, sleeping.

I sat down on the couch, lifted Tasha up on to my lap, and then answered the phone.

'Hello?'

Silence.

'Hello?'

If they don't identify themselves after the second hello, I always hang up. I hung up.

Tasha and I watched some old sit-coms on *Nick At Nite* and then I went in and got ready to go to bed, where Felice already was.

The phone rang again.

This time I picked it up on the nightstand next to the bed.

'Hello?'

Silence.

'Hello?'

Still nothing.

I hung up. Now Felice was propped up on one elbow, looking at me.

I shook my head. Don't answer.

Okay. She flattened herself under the cover again, but I didn't think she went back to sleep.

When I came out of the bathroom fifteen minutes later, my mouth smarting from the nuclear mouthwash I use, the phone rang once again.

This time when I picked up, I said nothing.

Finally, a woman said: 'Hello.'

'Who is this?'

'I'd like to speak with Mr Payne.'

'Who is this?'

Silence.

'My name is Eleanor Wilson. Ellie.'

'This is Robert Payne. Did you call here earlier?'

Hesitation. Then: 'Yes. I'm sorry. I shouldn't have hung up those times. I was just – nervous.'

'What can I do for you, Mrs Wilson?'

'You sound angry. I'm sorry we got off on the wrong foot.'

We always like to think that the beautiful ones are self-possessed and in control. She was anything but.

'I'm afraid to say – well, what I called to say.'

'I'm not an ogre, Mrs Wilson. Just say it.'

'Call me Ellie. Please.'

I sighed. 'Ellie, look. Why don't you just get to the point and then we'll see if there's any way I can help you.'

'You still sound angry.'

I whistled a couple bars of *Moon River*.

She laughed. 'I knew you'd have a sense of humor. I saw that in your eyes tonight. You know, at the rectory.'

'Now that I'm in such a good mood, Ellie, why don't you tell me why you called?'

'They'll think I did it, won't they?'

'The police?'

'Yes.'

'Think you killed Father Daly?'

Hesitation. 'You saw the earring when it fell out of my purse tonight.'

'Yes, I did.' Obviously I did. I picked it up. Was she on something?

I kept seeing her face, her beautiful beautiful face. I felt almost giddy, her ridiculously lovely fashion, my ridiculously painful loneliness despite Felice's presence. Ellie had me dreaming high school dreams, me with a nice new red convertible, squiring the Homecoming Queen around town.

Not that my life had ever been like that. The only convertible I'd ever owned had been a junker, and the Homecoming Queen of my senior year of high school had pronounced me a 'dip-shit' in front of maybe twenty people. She'd been wearing white fabric pumps that matched her gown. During her mercy slow dance with me I'd trod mightily on her toes.

'Bob said he knows you saw it – the other earring. Not the one in my purse, the one in the room. He knows you know he took it.'

'I kind've figured he did.'

'He'd be very angry if he knew I was talking to you.'

I sighed. 'I guess I'm not sure what you'd like me to do exactly, Ellie.'

'Meet for lunch tomorrow.'

'Lunch?'

'I need to talk to you. I may even hire you. We have plenty of money, if that's what you're concerned about.'

Her face again. Her grave wonderful eyes.

'Where would you like to meet?' I said.

'I was thinking of Thurber Park. There's a little restaurant down the street from the boat dock. They have good seafood.'

'I need to say something here, Ellie.'

'I know. You reserve the right to think that I'm guilty.'

'Yes. That's right.'

'My earring being there, I suppose your being suspicious is natural.'

'You were there last night with him, weren't you, Ellie?'

'I think I hear Bob pulling in. I need to go. I'll see you about noon tomorrow then.'

She hung up fast, and I sighed. I was out of the mood for sleep now. I went back to my spare-room table.

My cat Tasha came in and spent the next hour on my lap while I started working up the profile of Father Daly's killer and getting nowhere because I really didn't have enough data to work with.

The problem is that no matter what anybody tells you, psychological profiling is not a science. It's an art. It works well in some cases, but almost all of the cases it works for are sex-related crimes, which includes almost all serial killings. Even a contract killer has a *reason* he's willing to do that work. It's also relevant to other serial crimes, especially arson that's not for profit.

I wasn't sure I had a sex-related killing here. I wasn't sure I had a serial killing. If I did, I didn't know – or wasn't sure – what the prior crimes had been.

If only I'd found those clippings somewhere other than in the victim's room . . .

If wishes were horses, beggars would ride. If frogs had wings they wouldn't bump their butts when they hopped.

Felice came in twice for kisses, and I went out there once for a kiss, and then I was back at it.

When I heard the doorbell, the first thing I did was look at my wrist-watch on the table. It was late for visitors.

'I'll get that,' I called out.

If there was a crazy at the door, I wanted to be the one to greet him.

I stuffed my Luger into my pants pocket and walked through the apartment. Felice had given up on sleep. She was watching Jay Leno, clicking down the volume with the channel surfer.

I walked to the door and peeked out through the spyhole.

At first, I didn't recognize him. He looked just like any gray-haired and rather nondescript guy in his late sixties.

Then I realized who he was and my stomach knotted up immediately.

'Oh, shit,' I said.

'Is everything all right?' Felice said from the couch.

'I'll explain later.'

I opened up the door and the first thing he said was, 'Hey, I really like your new digs, Bobby. This is the kind of pad chicks love.'

New digs. Pad. Chicks.

I only knew one person, besides Gilhooley of course, who still talked this way. And it was a person I didn't ever want to see again.

I didn't know how he'd found me. But he always could get what he wanted. Even new addresses.

I made three quick assessments: he looked much older, and

had dropped maybe as much as fifty pounds. He was no longer a clothes horse; his sport jacket looked cheap and wrinkled, his chinos even worse. And he'd developed this very croupy cough. He stood in my doorway hacking and coughing.

Then I took full notice of the lone battered suitcase that sat next to him.

'Travelin' kind of light these days, Bobby,' he said.

'Is there something I can do for you, Vic?'

Then I became aware of his gasping. It was as if he couldn't suck in sufficient air.

'You could invite me in and let me sit down,' he panted.

'I'm sorry, Vic, but I don't want to invite you in.'

I started to close the door but then a slender, elegant hand touched mine and Felice whispered, 'This isn't like you, Robert. I've never seen you this mean before. That man is sick.'

She then pulled the door open again and said, 'Please, come in and sit down.'

For him, she had a smile, for me a glower.

'Why, thank you so much, ma'am.'

'I'm Felice,' she said, bending down to take his suitcase. 'I'm Robert's friend.'

'I'm Vic Carney,' he said. 'I'm Robert's stepfather.'

He moved very slowly, as if he were afraid he might pitch over at any time.

Felice helped him inside, and then made him a nice comfy place on the couch.

'How about a cup of hot chocolate?'

He grinned with cheap, store-bought teeth. 'That sounds great. You sure got yourself a nice gal, Bobby.'

I followed her out to the kitchen.

'How can you treat that sweet old man that way, Robert?'

'One, because he isn't a sweet old man, he's a con artist. And two, because—' I stopped. 'Never mind.'

She glared at me. 'Never mind?'

'He was an advertising guy. Worked for a couple of nickel

71

and dime agencies. After my father died, my mother was very vulnerable. But even so, I couldn't believe it when she took up with Vic. My father was a geologist, a very quiet, intelligent, honorable guy. Then here comes Vic, this advertising asshole. I couldn't believe it.

'He was always trying to impress me with how cool he was, how he played golf with the Governor, and knew a lot of the movie stars he used in his biggest commercials, and how he was making all this money. I tried never to take anything from him. If he bought me something, I always gave it back.'

She watched me quietly as I spoke. There was real rage in my voice and, I suspected, on my face.

'I hate to say this, Robert, but it sort of sounds like you hated him because he tried to take your father's place with you and your mother.'

'All those hours with the shrinks are starting to rub off on you. I hate him because he's a jerk.'

'I'm serious,' she said, as the milk came to a boil. She spooned chocolate powder into a cup. 'It sounds like you had more of a problem with him than he had with you.'

'Down deep, he's a used-car salesman,' I said. 'He's already got you conned. He was able to con almost anybody.'

'He conned your mother?'

'Absolutely. She was never able to see him for what he is.'

'But he didn't con you?'

'No, he didn't. I always knew what he was.'

She smiled. 'A pod person?'

'Exactly. A very dangerous pod person.' I paused. 'Plus, he took her away – everywhere. Europe, the South Seas, Russia . . . they were always traveling. I basically spent high school – after my dad died – alone.'

Felice plopped three small marshmallows into the hot drink and we went back to the living room. Vic was still hacking when we got there.

Felice gave him the drink then came over and put her nice bottom on the arm of the chair where I was sitting.

'So how long has it been since you two saw each other?' she said.

'Not long enough,' I said.

He'd been about to take a sip of his hot chocolate but when I spoke, he stopped, the cup halfway to his lips.

'Bobby hates me.'

'Oh, I'm sure he doesn't hate you,' she said.

He smiled grimly with his store-boughts. 'You don't hear him denying it, do you?'

'C'mon, Robert, tell Vic you don't hate him.'

I said nothing.

'I'm sorry, Vic,' she said. 'Bobby's just being an asshole. Some kind of male PMS deal or something like that.'

I couldn't help it. I laughed.

'See, he does know how to smile, Vic. Isn't that a cute little smile?'

'I probably wasn't a very good stepfather to him,' Vic said. 'I mean, I'm sure I could've handled things around the house much better. And I was kind of a showboat. Laura, his mother, I think she liked that about me. She liked all the advertising people, but Bobby always thought they were con artists. He read this Sloan Wilson novel where one of the characters said, "You don't go into advertising because you have talent; you go into advertising because you *don't* have talent." Bobby must've quoted that a hundred times at the dinner-table.'

Then he was coughing again. Violently.

Felice looked down at me, nodding her head angrily so I'd talk to him.

'Vic?'

'Just a minute, Bobby,' he managed to say between hacks.

'Vic, you want some Kleenex or something?'

'God dammit,' Felice whispered fiercely in my ear, 'you go over there and sit by him.'

I knew her moods well enough to know that this meant something to her. This wasn't an idle threat. Right now she saw me as a total shit and if I didn't extend myself at least a little bit to Vic she was going to take some permanent points away from me.

I'd never heard or seen anybody cough this way. He was totally caught up in it, as if in the throes of a seizure.

He dug a bottle of dark liquid out of his coat pocket and took two big swigs of the stuff.

He laid his head back against the couch and closed his eyes, apparently waiting for the liquid to take effect.

Felice was waving urgently for me to move closer to him.

I leaned over and said, 'You all right, Vic?'

His head came up slowly. Another store-bought smile. 'The doc said this stuff would help and I guess it does.'

Then he sat up straight and I went back to my own chair again.

'I guess I should come to the point, huh?'

'You just take your time,' Felice said. Stray puppies, cats, even raccoons, Felice had taken them all in at one time or another. Now she was taking in my stepfather. Or he was taking her in. Depends on how you mean the words.

He said, 'I have lung cancer and the docs give me about five, six months to live.'

'Oh, Lord, Vic. I'm sorry.' Then she said what most of us say in such situations. 'But you can never tell with those diagnoses they make. I mean, I know lots of people who're alive ten years after the doctors said they were going to die.'

We say things like that to make the sick person feel better. And we also say it to make ourselves feel better. It's a form of denial. Sure they've given you a terrible diagnosis but you're not going to die. And neither am I.

'I've seen the X-rays, kiddo,' he said gently. 'I think their diagnosis is probably pretty accurate.' He talked about going through chemo, and how lonely and scared and weak he'd been.

And then he started sobbing. And somewhere between the sobs, he started coughing again, too.

He buried his face in his hands.

Felice went over and sat on one side of him then gestured

wildly for me to come over and sit on the other side of him, which I did only reluctantly.

'Oh Vic,' she said, as he continued to cry. She held him like a baby, rocking him back and forth, back and forth.

I still couldn't feel anything but a kind of abstract sympathy for him. I wanted to. You couldn't look at the poor bastard and not feel sorry for him. But I couldn't open myself up. I was still a teenager missing his father, and he was still my swaggering, arrogant stepfather.

I wanted to say something comforting, but I couldn't.

Maybe I really was a shit after all.

ii

Not a fun night.

For one thing, both Felice and I were intimidated about making love with Vic right down the hall in the den.

For another, Felice spent her time, in between kisses, telling me how I had to be nice to Vic.

She'd definitely found another stray to adopt.

When the alarm woke me at seven, I was groggy, muscle-tired and cranky.

Male PMS, as Felice would call it.

The bed was empty.

I put on a robe and walked down the hall.

At the edge of the living room, I paused, listened.

The kitchen. Conversation. The morning radio show I usually listened to.

And the delicious smell of breakfast.

Apparently sensing that I was nearby, Vic leaned out of the kitchen doorway and saw me.

He wore street clothes and one of Felice's frilly aprons, and waved a good morning spatula at me.

'Speak of the devil, Felice. Look who's here.'

Then Felice appeared in her buff blue robe. She's one of those women who looks pretty damned good in the morning. 'Hi, hon,' she said. 'Vic's making us breakfast.'

And he's also making himself at home, I thought.

But that was obviously the plan. His plan. And most likely her plan, too.

I almost said something to him about being so presumptuous. But then he started hacking, and what the hell was I going to say to that? At least he turned his head away and didn't cough on our food.

We ate at the dining-room table that Felice had decorated brightly. 'Was the rollaway comfortable?' she asked Vic as we ate the scrambled eggs and French pancakes he'd made. He'd always been a good cook. I remembered being twelve and resenting him for that particular skill. My father had been one of those guys who couldn't even successfully navigate a hamburger. But there was my mother swooning over Vic's prowess with the grill and the hibachi.

'Just great, Felice. You fixed it up real nice for me.'

Every time Vic put his head down to eat, Felice'd do one of her nodding jobs again. Like: go ahead, talk to him. I knew I'd be in trouble if I didn't.

'So,' I said, 'can I give you a ride somewhere this morning, Vic?' I was hinting that I wanted him to settle in someplace else.

She kicked me.

And I mean, she *kicked* me. Hard.

'Vic and I plan to go to the city market and get some fresh vegetables for tonight,' she said. 'Vic knows this great casserole recipe.'

'It's vegetarian, Bobby,' he said.

Another kick. 'Isn't that nice, honey? The fact that it's vegetarian?'

'Yeah,' I said. 'That's nice.'

'You all right, Bobby?' Vic said.

'Huh?'

'You keep wincing.'

'Oh,' I said, 'just a little pain I have in my leg.'

Not to mention the pain in my ass, I thought, looking over at the beaming Felice.

'We're also going to do a little clothes shopping,' Felice said.

'We are?' Vic said.

'Uh-huh. Your clothes are a little too big for you.'

'Aw, Felice, I don't have that kind of money. Fact is, and I may as well be honest about it, I spent all my money right before I was diagnosed. After Bobby's mother died . . . well, I kind of went through a second childhood again. I bought a Vette and started hitting the bottle pretty hard and . . . well, anyway, what I'm trying to say is that I'm broke and it's not anybody's fault but mine, and I certainly didn't come here looking for charity.'

'It isn't charity,' Felice said. 'I get tired of hanging around here all the time alone. You can be my paid companion.'

He smiled. 'Like a gigolo?'

'Exactly like a gigolo,' she giggled. 'It'll be fun, won't it, Robert?'

She was able to find the exact same spot on my leg three times in a row. She had a foot that was as accurate as a heat-seeking missile.

'Oh yeah,' I said, 'you two'll have a great time.'

He gave me one of his ad-man winks. 'I have to warn you, Bobby, I'm going to do everything I can to steal her away from you.'

I don't know why but it pissed me off, what he said, and the way he said it. He was always the slickie, always the hustler, even when his lungs were giving out on him.

Felice seemed to sense how unhappy I was. She touched my hand and looked at me and said, 'I'm afraid you don't have any chance of stealing me, Vic. Robert here's my one true love.'

I appreciated what she said – she was a tender and loving woman, Felice was – but it didn't make me any happier about this whole situation.

I took a quick shower and kissed Felice goodbye.

Vic was in her bathroom.

She walked me to the door. 'This'll work out, hon. You'll see.'

Then she kissed me and it was a warm and wonderful kiss.

But it didn't change my feelings any.

'No, it won't,' I said. 'I hate that prick and I always will.'

In the car, I called the police department and asked for Detective Judy Holloway.

After I identified myself, she said, 'I still can't get over a priest using a French tickler.'

She had herself a war story that she'd be able to tell for years.

'So how can I help you this morning, Mr Payne?'

'There are two murders I'm interested in.'

'Oh?'

I described the murders and gave her the dates. 'I wonder if you could fax me the preliminary reports.'

'I suppose I could, Mr Payne, but now you're making me curious.'

'Oh?'

'Why would you suddenly be interested in these two cases?'

'Monsignor Gray asked me to just sniff around a little.'

' "Sniff around" meaning what exactly?'

'Exactly, I'm not sure. I think he just needs to feel that everybody is doing everything they can to find the killer.'

'We *are* doing everything we can, Mr Payne.'

'I'm aware of that. I really am. And I told him so.'

'Let me ask you something, Mr Payne.'

'All right?'

'Is there any evidence you're withholding?'

I thought about the earring. I hadn't been expecting a question like this. If I told Detective Holloway about the earring now, I could have some legal difficulties on my hands.

'Nothing I can think of,' I said.

'Now there's a forthright answer.'

'I'm just trying to help my friend.'

'And *I'm* just trying to help your friend.' She sighed. 'Do you have a fax number?'

I gave it to her.

'The preliminary report is the only thing I can release.'

'I understand and I appreciate it.'

'It'd be fun to get you under oath some time, Mr Payne.'

I laughed. 'Fun for you, maybe.'

'It's only in movies that private eyes get involved in murder investigations, Mr Payne.'

'Not anymore, Detective Holloway. One of the first people a good criminal attorney hires these days is a field investigator. And most of us are licensed by the state as private operatives.'

'And yours was issued three-and-a-half years ago following the death of your wife and your resignation from the FBI.'

'You checked me out.'

'Just doing my job, Mr Payne.'

'I don't blame you at all.'

'That's nice of you.' Then: 'Chew around the edges if you want to, Mr Payne, but don't try to hide anything from me. Understood?'

'Understood.'

'You wouldn't want to piss me off. Believe me.'

'I believe you.'

'I'll fax those reports over to you. Have a nice day, Mr Payne.'

It took me most of the morning but I eventually located Paul Gaspard.

He lived in a red-brick six-plex in the middle of a block that had started turning black a few years ago. A variety of dirty words had been painted on the west wall of the apartment building and most of the windows were cracked and several of the cheap aluminum doors showed dents where burglar bars had been used to jimmy them open.

Gaspard lived on the second floor. Two little black faces peering around the edge of a curtain stared at me all the time I stood in front of Gaspard's door and knocked. I waved at them and grinned. They looked at each other as if they weren't sure how to respond. Then one of them waved at me. And then the other one did, too.

Gaspard opened the door on three different chain locks. 'Yeah?'

'I'd like to talk to you about finding Father Daly.'

'I already talked to you fellas. You woke me up.'

'I'm sorry I woke you, Mr Gaspard. But I'm not police. I'm a legal investigator working for Monsignor Gray.'

'Legal investigator? What the hell's that?'

I explained it as cogently as I could.

'Shit,' he said. 'I guess you might as well come in. You got me woke up now.'

The apartment was small, cluttered and smelled of cigarette smoke and greasy food. For most of the time I was there, a tiny Pekingese stood in front of me and yipped. He had a cute little collar with his name, MIGHTY MIKE, spelled out on it with fake rubies.

Gaspard looked to be in his mid-sixties, a balding man with liver spots on both his hands and his face. He was thin but it was an unhealthy thin. I wondered if he'd been sick. He wore a once-white T-shirt, gray work pants and felt slippers with the toes cut out.

He said, 'He was dead when I got there.'

'All right.'

'And I didn't see anything or hear anything.'

'You checked him in?'

'Uh-huh.'

'When?'

'You want some instant coffee?'

'No, thanks.'

'I'm going to have one. I just can't get started without a little coffee.'

The kitchenette, as they are called, was just big enough to fit a small stove and refrigerator in the corner. Gaspard took a battered saucepan, filled it with water, then stood there to wait while it boiled.

'I checked him in just after midnight.'

'Had he checked into your motel before?'

He paused. Then shook his head. 'That priest got more ass than a toilet seat as we used to say.'

'So you'd checked him in before?'

'Usually once or twice a week. He usually wore a hat and dark glasses and kept his collar up, but I always knew who he was.'

'You ever see any of the women he was with?'

Gaspard shook his head. 'He was real cagey about that. He'd have them park in back so they could walk right to his room without me seeing them.'

'But you're sure he always had somebody with him?'

'Why would a man rent a room to be alone?'

You ask a stupid question, you get a stupid answer.

Gaspard brought his coffee over and sat back down in his recliner. His lime-green recliner. The couch I sat on was orange crushed velvet. The crushed velvet ottoman was light blue. Being color blind was apparently one of Gaspard's virtues.

'Did Father Daly act any different than usual that night?'

'Different how?'

'You know, scared or more talkative or less talkative or—'

He sipped his coffee. 'He looked – nervous or something.'

'Why do you think that?'

'He walked over to the window a couple of times while I was getting him his key. He stared outside like he was trying to see if somebody had followed him.'

'Maybe he was looking for his woman.'

'Don't think so.'

'Oh?'

'Like I said, the women always came around back.'

'You ever see him nervous like that before?'

'Huh-uh. And it gave me a funny feeling.'

'Funny feeling?'

'Yeah. I used to get that in Nam. And I mean Nam when it was rough. Sixty-four and sixty-five. Before Johnson decided to give the grunts any air cover.'

I looked at the framed photographs hanging above the dusty Formica table that had been shoved against the living-room wall. Gaspard young, with and without his parents; Gaspard in his thirties, in uniform and in Nam; and Gaspard in a bowling shirt about to roll an important ball. Most women seem able to make a hovel appear home-like. But not men. This place writhed with loneliness and boredom and drift. No matter how many years he lived here, it would always feel temporary. I guess that's why the dog kept yipping. The place was getting to him.

'Anyway, six, seven guys I went over with got killed there. And right before they did, I always got this funny feeling about them. You ever see any TV shows about ESP?'

'A few.'

'I think that's maybe what it was. That funny feeling, I mean.'

'And you had the same sort of feeling about Father Daly?'

'Exactly.'

'As if something bad was going to happen to him?'

'Uh-huh.'

'You say that to him?'

'Say it to him?' He looked at me as if I was profoundly stupid. 'I never let him know I knew who he was.'

'I see.'

'He gave me Communion sometimes over at St Mallory's Church, but if he knew who I was, he never let on.'

'But the other night—'

'I know what you'd like me to say but I can't say it because it wouldn't be true.'

'You didn't see or hear—'

'I didn't see or hear anything.' Then: 'Oh, I forgot. About the phone call.'

'The phone call?'

'Yeah.'

'When was this?'

'Maybe one, one-fifteen, something like that.'

'It came to the switchboard—'

'Came to the switchboard – it's just a little board we've got – and I put it through to the room.'

'Father Daly answered?'

'I assume he did.'

'Tell me about the caller. Male?'

'I think so. It was pretty muffled. They'd put something across the phone, whoever it was.'

'What did he say?'

'Said he wanted to be connected with Room 154.'

'So he knew the room number?'

'Yes.'

'Was that the room number Father Daly usually had?'

'That or Room 152 or 156. The rooms on the back wall. He always wanted one of them.'

'So you connected him and that was the last you heard from the caller.'

'Right.' Then: 'Mike. C'mon now, Mr Payne is our guest.'

Mighty Mike was yipping and yapping and driving me crazy. Every time I tried to reach down and pet him, he snarled at me with spiky little vampiric teeth.

Mighty Mike was reminding me why I was a cat man.

'I got to get up and get going,' Gaspard said. 'Got my line-dancing lessons in the afternoon. The gal I go out with is kind of heavy.' He smiled with cheap, gleaming dentures. 'But I figure she likely never went out with nobody as bad-lookin' as me, so we're probably even up.'

There was a sadness and humility in his words that made me like him suddenly. He was a decent man, and an honorable one.

'I'd like to leave my card with you.'

'I've told you everything I know, Mr Payne. But if you want to leave your card, fine.'

I stood up, took out a card, carried it over to his recliner.

'Just in case,' I said, handing it to him.

Mighty Mike walked me to the door, snarling at me all the way.

'He's really a good dog,' Gaspard said.

'Yeah, I can see that.'

The two little boys were still in the window when I left. This time they waved first.

I smiled and waved back.

Even when I was all the way down to the sidewalk, I could hear Mighty Mike still yipping.

iii

COUNTY OF LINN, INVESTIGATOR'S REPORT
Department of Medical Examiner
620-3764
Homicide
CRPD/Evans
INFORMATION SOURCE:
Detectives Miles and Reynolds
LOCATION:
Bowker Park
INVESTIGATION:
620-3764 A 31-year-old black female is the victim of an apparent homicide.
STATEMENTS:
According to Detective Miles, a woman in the park was looking for her dog when she came upon the body of the deceased.

The decedent was last seen alive at the Suds 'N Brew tavern at approx. 8:15 P.M. on the previous evening.
SCENE DESCRIPTION/BODY EXAMINATION:
I arrived at the scene at 0805 hr. The body was lying between two jack pine trees near the northwest end of the park.

Decedent was lying on her back. She wore a plaid skirt, pantyhose, a white frilly blouse and a brown winter coat. From appearances, she did not appear to have been sexually assaulted. Her white cloth underwear showed no evidence of semen or blood.

The most obvious wounds were a) several stab wounds in the area of her heart and b) her eyes, which somebody had crudely dug out of their sockets.

Rigor mortis was fully established.

More than six fresh footprints were discovered near and around the decedent.

EVIDENCE:

620-3765: Hair standards and fingernail standards were taken.

620-3766: Hair and nail standards taken as well as physical evidence by criminologist B. P. Jepsen.

IDENTIFICATION/NOTIFICATION:

620-3767: Identification was established at scene by husband Thomas being summoned to the park. He identified wife immediately.

When I finished with that report, I started in on the second, wanting to refresh my memory. The report concerned a Ronald Swanson, age fifty-six. He, too, had been stabbed, though the clinical reports about the type of weapon and condition of the knife blade indicated that two very different weapons had been used.

Probably because I felt guilty (and somewhat unprofessional) about withholding the earring from her, Detective Holloway was my first call.

'It's like we're going steady now,' she said, after I identified myself. 'I mean, you call every twenty minutes it seems like.'

'Well, you are kind of cute now that you mention it.'

'So are you, Mr Payne. But I'm a happily married gal with three kids.'

'Three kids? You don't look any older than thirty.'

'Boy, save some of that butter for popcorn at the movies.'

I laughed. There's a certain type of wise-ass woman who is even funnier than a wise-ass man. Holloway was one of them.

'Now let's be serious,' I said.

'Fine by me.'

'Tawanna Jackson had her eyes cut out, right?'

'Right.'

'And Ronald Swanson had his ear cut off, right?'

'Right.'

'And now Father Daly's had his tongue cut out, right?'

'Right. But what does it mean?'

'Seeing, hearing, speaking.'

'I'm just a country girl, Mr Payne, not a high-powered FBI-type like yourself.'

'See no evil, hear no evil, speak no evil. The Three Wise Monkeys.'

Silence. Then: 'I'll be damned.'

'You buy it?'

'I don't know if I buy it, Mr Payne, but I've got to give you an A for imagination.' Then: 'It is kind of interesting at that. You have any theories as to how these three people tie in together?'

'St Mallory's.'

'Right. But that's the obvious one, Mr Payne. St Mallory's a big church. And they were all stabbed. But you know how many murder victims are stabbed to death every year? Any other connection?'

'I don't know. But I think that between us we should be able to find one.'

'If one exists,' she said.

'Right. If one exists.'

'See no evil, hear no evil, speak no evil. It does sort of make sense.'

'You work on it, and so will I.'

Then: 'The captain is waving at me, Mr Payne. I'd better see what he wants.'

'I appreciate you taking me seriously.'

'Why, that's all right, Mr Payne. But I don't take you half as seriously as you and your FBI buddies take yourselves.'

She said it in the sweetest of ways, and then hung up. I wondered just what kind of bad experience she'd had with the Bureau in the past.

But then most city cops feel that way.

iv

Gilhooley reached me on my car phone.

'I got something for you, Robert. But I'm not sure what it means yet.'

'Yeah? What is it?'

'It seems your friend Ellie Wilson's got one hell of a temper. A social worker accused her of four different counts of child abuse. But nobody ever brought any charges against her.'

'Physical abuse?'

'Yeah – very bad physical abuse. Broken ribs, black eyes – things like that. Seems elegant Ellie was brought up by a very religious mother. And Ellie really freaks out when she thinks her kids have been "bad." She's judge and jury.'

'Good work. I'm going to be seeing Ellie in a little bit, matter of fact.'

'Don't say anything dirty. She might slug you.'

We hung up.

Gilhooley tells me that if you want really great cuisine you need to go to Iowa City. But then Maoists aren't known for their gourmet tastes.

In former days, downtown Cedar Rapids was crowded with good little restaurants offering the standard fare of seafood and steak. Ethnic restaurants, at that time, didn't have much chance of success.

But over the past ten years, ethnic food has become one of

the mainstays of Cedar Rapids restaurants. Indian, Chinese, German, Greek, French and Korean fare have done especially well out here. Of course, this has happened simultaneously with Cedar Rapids itself becoming more cosmopolitan. On sunny streets these days, you hear a variety of languages spoken, from Japanese to French to Lebanese. And at the rate Cedar Rapids is adding international businesses, there will be even more languages spoken very soon.

The place where I was to meet Ellie Wilson was a block away from a large downtown park. At noontime, the restaurant was crowded with workers from the various office buildings. There was an old joke about Cedar Rapids. Hold your middle finger up and say, 'You know what this is?'

'No, what's that?'

'The Cedar Rapids skyline.'

This was when we had only one building taller than fifteen stories. Now we have several so the joke no longer applies. There are now enough people working downtown to pack the restaurants every single working day.

I left my name with the hostess and took a table next to a window where I could watch the river. I was on my second cup of coffee when I looked up and saw Ellie Wilson.

'I'm sorry I'm late.'

'I'm in no particular hurry.'

She was breathless as she sat down. 'I think he's following me.'

'Who is following you?'

'Bob. My husband.'

'Why would he follow you?'

She was about to say more when the waiter appeared.

'My name is Phil and I'll be your waiter today. Would you care for something from the bar?'

I've always felt that name tags were sufficient. That way, knowing the waiter's name is elective. If I was all that curious about it, I could look up at the plastic rectangle riding his shirt pocket and see his name for myself. At least he wasn't dressed up like a pirate or anything.

'I'll have a glass of white wine,' Ellie Wilson said. White was the motif for the day. She wore a white suit that gave her an open, summery look.

'That sounds good, plus a cup of coffee,' I said.

After our pal Phil left, she said, 'He's been following me the last couple of months.'

'Any special reason?'

'He thought I was having an affair.'

'Were you?'

'Yes. Yes, I was. I'm ashamed to admit it, but it's the truth.'

She glanced around the restaurant, as if somebody might be eavesdropping on our conversation. The place was a large room filled with small tables covered with starchy white tablecloths and centered with fretted black metal candle-holders. There was a hungry mob waiting up by the cash register. They wanted us to hurry the hell up and eat and get out of there.

'And you think he followed you today?'

'Yes. In fact, I know he did. I think I lost him but it was only about five or six blocks ago.'

'Would this have anything to do with Father Daly?'

Phil had great timing.

'White wine for the lady, white wine for the gentleman,' he said, setting down our drinks. 'And another cup of coffee, too.'

Every once in a while I catch myself being the grinch. I had no right to be irritated with Phil. He was pleasant and professional and he obviously worked damned hard for his money.

'Thanks, Phil,' I said when he was done.

'You're most welcome,' he said as he turned to walk away.

Eleanor sipped her wine. She had long, elegant fingers. Every once in a while you're in the presence of a woman who nudges you off your normal orbit. You feel yourself drawn into her orbit and there's nothing you can do about it.

'You were going to tell me about Father Daly.'

She sighed. 'It sounds pretty low-rent.'

'That's all right.'

'One more sip of wine.' She had a sad crushing smile. 'I come from a family of alcoholics. I'm always afraid that's how I'll end up some day.' She looked at me with eyes clear as first light. 'But you want to know about Father Daly and me.'

A brief sigh. 'Bob and I were having some problems. This was two years ago. I went to a therapist but I just didn't care for her all that much. She wanted to run my life and I resented it. Anyway, I had a friend who was seeing Father Daly. She was very happy with him. He seemed to have done her a lot of good. He was a very good therapist, he really was. No platitudes, no stupid little theories. He saw my faults and Bob's faults very clearly. And then he started falling in love with me.'

'Father Daly?'

'Uh-huh. I mean, every session, he'd find some way to touch me.'

'You mean sexually?'

'That's what it was all about. At first I was kind of scared, and then I was kind of flattered. And then one day, I realized that I was attracted to him, too. Not as strongly as he was to me – but there was a definite attraction there.'

'Your husband didn't sense anything between you and Father Daly?'

'Not then. There wasn't anything *to* sense, for one thing. It was sort of like puppy love. At least for me. He was a very good-looking man and very polished, and very witty. He made me laugh. He even told me an Andrew Marvell line about that. You know, the poet?'

'Yes.'

' "The maid who laughs is half taken," he said to me one day. And I knew he was talking about our relationship.'

'Did you stop seeing him?'

'Yes. For about three months. He'd call several times a week. He was – obsessed with me, I think.'

'How were things going at home?'

'Not all that well.' She had some more wine. 'Bob was still angry with me. He sensed that our marriage would never be the way it once had been.'

'Why not?'

'He was unfaithful to me for years. No serious affairs, nothing like that. But there were always these little dollies he was sneaking off with. A lot of my friends' husbands are like that, but the women don't seem to care all that much. Boys will be boys, that sort of thing. But it took its toll on me. He'd come home drunk and smelling of them and finally it killed something inside me. I'd had a very unhappy affair in college. It took me two years to get over it. That was when I met Bob.

'He was a year younger than me but he was a big football star – he set a Big Ten rushing record that year – and I saw him as this magical man. He was going to make things all better for me. We got married as soon as he graduated from college. And I started having babies right away. Three daughters in five years. That's when Bob began to drift away. I was at home barefoot and pregnant and he was out chasing after his little dollies. It's a pretty typical middle-class story, at least for my generation. My daughters would never put up with it, thank God. They're much tougher than my generation was.'

'Ready to see menus?' Phil said.

We saw menus. She had the seafood special, I had the seafood special.

'I'm sorry I'm talking so much,' she said, after Phil left.

'That's why we're here. To talk.'

'But I must admit, it feels good.'

'So you started seeing Father Daly again?'

'Yes. About three months ago. Bob had begun to sense that I really didn't love him any more, and he was looking for a reason. He became paranoid – very suspicious. That's when he started following me. Sometimes I'd even hear him pick up the extension phone when I was talking with one of my girlfriends.'

'He didn't know about Father Daly?'

'Oh, he knew I was seeing him in a professional capacity, but I don't think he knew – how Father Daly felt about me.'

She saw him before I did. She said, 'Oh, God.'

'What?'

Suddenly husband Bob was at the table, yanking me to my feet with my necktie. And suddenly husband Bob was bellowing for wife Ellie to get the hell out of here and get the hell back home where she belonged.

And suddenly Phil, poor dumb Phil, made the mistake of coming over and saying, 'Is everything all right?'

Bob punched him, hard enough to draw blood from one side of his nose.

Two thoughts came to me – one, that good old Bob would probably get around to punching me very soon, too – and two, that I was now the most-watched person in the entire restaurant. Except perhaps for husband Bob.

I brought my left foot up and stomped on his instep. In his first moment of pain, I brought my right knee up and caught him squarely in the groin.

His body wasn't sure what to do. So much sharp pain so quickly.

He stood there and looked at me, all very executive in his three-piece blue business suit, and then he started to fold in half, giving way to the pain.

'Here, Phil,' I said, grabbing the napkin and putting it to his nose. 'Go put some cold water on it.'

By now, Ellie had fled the restaurant. The last I'd seen of her was her back.

'You sonofabitch,' Bob said as he began to compose himself. 'You stay away from her. In case you hadn't noticed, she's a married woman.' He was still grimacing from the pain.

I took two twenties from my wallet and laid them down next to my plate.

'I owe you one, asshole,' he said as I started to walk away from the table. 'And believe me, I'm going to pay you back.'

By now, the other diners had given up their furtive looks.

They'd quit eating entirely and were watching us openly, boldly, the way they'd watch a soap opera.

'And you're supposed to be helping with the murder investigation,' he said. 'So why the hell aren't you out trying to find the killer instead of hitting on my wife?'

I've always been self-conscious in front of groups. And I'd never felt more self-conscious than in front of this particular group.

I looked straight ahead at the door and then started walking toward it as fast as I could.

Only when I got outside, away from all the curious eyes, did I realize that I hadn't asked Ellie Wilson the most important question of all.

What the hell *had* her earring been doing in Father Daly's motel room last night?

In my hurry to leave the apartment this morning, I'd forgotten some papers I needed for the law office. When I stopped by my place, Felice's Jaguar was parked in the lot.

I expected to hear voices when I opened the apartment door, but I heard nothing.

'Hello?' I said. 'Hello?'

Felice suddenly appeared in the hallway, holding a *shushing* finger to her lips.

'What's the matter?' I said.

She shook her lovely head and whispered, 'I just got him to sleep.'

'Is something wrong with him?'

She cocked her head back and glared at me. 'No, Jack, everything is just peachy with him. He only has a case of terminal lung cancer is all.'

'You know god-damned well what I meant,' I said. 'Did something happen?'

She sighed. Shook her head again. She continued to whisper. 'We went shopping. But all of a sudden he really started hacking and he got so tired he had to sit down. He had to sit there for an hour before he could even walk a little bit. It took me another twenty minutes to get him in the car. I got him home and called the hospital. A nurse told me that this was typical of lung cancer, getting so tired and everything, and that I should put him to bed.'

Now it was my turn to glare. 'You're not as devious as you think.'

'Boy, that doesn't sound too paranoid, Robert. What the hell's that supposed to mean?'

'It means that I still don't like the sonofabitch. I've been thinking about it and I don't want him staying here.'

'He doesn't have any money, Robert.'

'Yeah – and you know *why* he doesn't have any money? Because he drank it all up with his advertising buddies, that's why.' I moved closer to her. 'He's not going to stay here, Felice.'

'Maybe I could fix him up a place in the parking lot. You know, by the dumpster or something. Would that make you happy?'

'You won't have to. I'm going to find him a nursing home and I'm going to pick up the tab and that's the last I want to see of the sonofabitch. You can visit him if you want to but don't expect me to go along.'

'I don't want to see you right now, Robert. I can't believe you're acting like this.'

'Well, right now, I don't particularly want to see *you* either,' I said, and walked over to the front door.

'Maybe I'll get a place for me and Vic to stay,' she said.

'Fine by me.'

' "Fine by me." You should see yourself, Robert. You look like a hateful little boy right at this moment.'

'Well, maybe that's what I am, Felice. Maybe that's my true nature.'

And with that, I left my apartment.

I was two blocks away before I realized that I hadn't picked up the papers I needed for the office.

But there was no way I was going to go another couple of rounds with Felice.

Not right now, anyway.

As I drove, and tried to concentrate on the road, I felt isolated and very, very sorry for myself.

Vic shows up and displaces me from my own apartment.

I no longer had a home.

At least, that was how I felt.

Then my cell phone rang.

I picked up.

'I love you, Robert,' she said.

'Who is this?'

'Very funny.'

I sighed. 'I'm sorry I was such a jerk.'

'I was a jerk, too. I just feel sorry for him, Robert.'

'Yeah.'

'But now I feel I'm being disloyal to you.'

'We'll work it out.'

'I really do love you.'

I smiled. 'I really do love you, too.'

3:

POLICE DEPARTMENT

Michael James Grady
Age: 34
Race: Caucasian
Occupation: High School Teacher
Marital Status: M
Military Service: None

Grady: You're making this a lot worse than it is. I mean, right now there's all this politically correct bullshit on the subject . . . but the fact is, you look at any society you want to name . . . and it happens in every one of them. Now I'll admit, the time I accidentally pushed her down the stairs . . . well, I got carried away. I mean, I certainly didn't plan to break her arm. It just happened. I gave her a little push and . . . and the same for the time she miscarried. I was pretty drunk and I gave her a shove. I meant to shove her shoulder . . . but I guess I must have hit her stomach . . . and hit it pretty hard. I have to admit, it scared the shit out of me. She's been talking about making me see this counselor, but she knows if she pushes that particular line any more, I'm out the door. Teachers have enough grief to contend with these days . . . rumors start spreading that I'm a quote, unquote, wife beater . . . I'll be out of a job. And you can bet your ass on that.

Michael Grady

Wakes up in the morning and of course it's the first thing he remembers. What he did last night.

In the upper bunk, his college roomie is, as usual, snoring his ass off. Roomie is going to flunk out of the university here if he doesn't get his ass in gear.

Puts one foot then the other on the floor and then stands up.

The room is a pit. Grady is reasonably clean and neat but McGrath is a pig. God, how can anybody who came from a family as wealthy as McGrath's stand to live this way?

Pizza boxes all over the floor, dirty underwear dangling off the arms of chairs, Pepsi bottles filled with cigarette butts.

God.

The hangover hits him now full force.

He feels dehydrated and sick to his stomach.

And the memories keep coming back.

God, did it really happen?

Did he really do it?

He stumbles toward the john, his foot brushing against a piece of cold pizza on the floor. It looks like chunky barf. The sight of it makes him think maybe *he's* going to barf.

He pisses, rocking on his heels as he does so. He keeps trying to will images of last night from his mind. But they won't go away.

He did it again, didn't he?

After all her warnings.

After all their arguments.

He went and did it again.

If only she hadn't . . .

He stumbles back out of the john to the little refrigerator McGrath keeps in the corner, right under the *Saturday Night Fever* poster.

They have this running battle, Grady and McGrath. Grady thinks John Travolta is the ultimate nerd. McGrath not only thinks otherwise . . . he even dresses like Travolta . . . the three-piece white suit and everything. It is 1979 and Travolta is God.

The thing is, John Travolta is this tall, skinny, handsome, street-wise guy.

Todd McGrath, on the other hand, is this short (5"5'), round (220 pounds), pimpled farm kid whose parents just happen to be filthy rich.

When he bends over to open the refrigerator door, some invisible somebody stabs a butcher knife right into the middle of his forehead.

The headache is so bad he's literally blinded.

He has to put a hand flat against the wall to keep from falling over.

God Almighty, he really did it last night.

Finally he's able to lean down and grab a can of Pepsi from the refrigerator.

He takes the Pepsi and the phone into the bathroom. The phone has an extra long cord. Whenever they want to talk in private, they take the phone into the john. Nothing like a toilet to inspire romance.

Confirm that it really happened. That's what he needs to do.

And if it *did* really happen, maybe it wasn't as bad as he thinks.

Maybe it was just a little lover's spat and not a big deal at all.

He puts the phone on the edge of the sink and then starts gunning the Pepsi.

As he drinks, he becomes aware of the smell of vomit.

Maybe he barfed last night and doesn't remember. Or maybe McGrath barfed. McGrath always barfs. He mixes beer and wine and, man, that'll make you sicker than anything.

He wishes he'd brought *two* Pepsis in with him. He's halfway done with this one and he's still dehydrated.

He turns to the phone and dials. His whole right arm is trembling.

Maybe it was *worse* than he remembers.

What if he really *hurt* her . . .

Her bitch roommate answers. Molly and Grady have this mutual loathing for each other. She thinks that Tina should have dumped Grady long ago and Grady thinks somebody should have *drowned* Molly long ago.

'Is Tina there?'

'It's early.'

'That isn't what I asked you. I asked you if she was there.'

'You sonofabitch. You did it to her again, didn't you?'

'It's none of your fucking business.'

So it really did happen after all . . .

'One of these times she's going to call the police. And if she doesn't, maybe *I* will.'

'Put her on the phone.'

'You prick.'

She lets the receiver drop to the desk. It bangs hard, the sudden sharp sound only increasing his headache.

Then she's back: 'She doesn't want to talk to you.'

'Bullshit. That's what you told her to say.'

'Look, Michael. She doesn't want to talk to you, all right? Those are her words, not mine.'

'Tell her if she doesn't talk to me, then I'll come over.'

'You bastard.'

Once again, the phone is dropped. Once again, a laser of pain shoots into his ear, and then angles up into the front of his head.

Then: 'Hello.'

He gets all corny inside. Can't help it. Just hearing her

voice after they've had a terrible fight . . . well, her voice just melts him.

'I'm sorry about last night.'

'It's over, Michael.'

'Oh God, Tina, we just had a little fight.'

'That isn't what the doctor told me.'

'Doctor? What the hell are you talking about?'

A pause. 'After you dropped me off last night, Molly had to take me to the emergency room. They did X-rays. You gave me a concussion last night, Michael. When you hit me in the head those times.'

Now the silence belongs to him. Then, finally: 'God, I didn't hit you that hard.'

'Well, you figure it out, Michael. You hit me in the head five times with your fist and now I have a concussion. That sounds pretty hard to me.'

'But Tina—'

'None of your bullshit, Michael. It's over.' He's never heard her like this. So cold. So self-confident. Usually, after he hits her, what she does is cry and say that maybe they shouldn't see each other any more but they always go back.

This time, though . . .

'What I should do is go to the police.'

'I love you, Tina.'

'Molly says I could press charges. She's in pre-law, so she knows what she's talking about.'

'I'll never do it again, I promise.'

'I wasn't even looking at him. That's what *really* pisses me off about this whole thing. You kept saying I was flirting with this guy at the bar but I couldn't even see anybody that far away, Michael. I didn't have my glasses on and I hadn't worn my contacts. I couldn't even *see* this guy you said I was flirting with.'

'I'll be better, Tina. I promise. I honest-to-God promise.'

'You'll have to be better with somebody else, Michael. I'm not going to see you any more. I'll have somebody bring all your stuff by.'

'Oh, God, Tina, please, please give me another chance.'

Now to his headache and nausea, add panic. She really sounds serious. She really is dumping me. Forever.

Oh my God.

'Goodbye, Michael.'

'But I love you, Tina. Doesn't that mean anything?'

'Yeah, you love me all right. You've hit me six different times in the past six months, Michael. You get these paranoid fantasies that I'm making it with somebody behind your back, and then you think you have the right to beat me up. No more, Michael. No more.'

Then she does the worst thing of all: hangs up quietly.

If she'd yelled at him . . . or banged the phone down in his ear . . . that would mean she was mad, and that she'd likely get over it.

But hanging up quietly . . . it has a finality about it that makes his arms break out in goosebumps.

She's gone from him and he knows it . . . gone.

Then there's a sudden and terrible pounding on the door.

'Hey, man! I gotta piss!'

And it's the one little thing that pushes Grady over the edge . . .

Oh, he opens the door all right but as soon as he sees Todd 'John Travolta' McGrath . . . Grady goes berserk.

In blinding seconds, he smashes a right hook into McGrath's face, then delivers a cracking left to the stomach . . . and then he slams the lard-ass back against the wall and puts two more punches into his face.

McGrath is crying and screaming like a girl, all hunched over in this pathetic posture that he thinks will stop him from being punched again.

But Grady is done with McGrath and turns back to the bathroom and the black telephone resting on the white sink.

He picks up the phone, jerks the cord taut, and then rips the cord from the wall.

Then he takes the phone and hurls it into the shower.

Somewhere out there, McGrath is still blubbering like a

girl. But Grady doesn't give a shit. All he can think of is how Tina just broke up with him.

All women are bitches. Every fucking one of them. Every fucking one.

Then suddenly he's bending over the toilet bowl and barfing his guts up.

Fucking bitches.

Every fucking one of them.

Three

i

In the last century, we were a nation of boarding houses. Read any literature on the assassination of Abraham Lincoln, and you'll find that many of the people alleged to be involved lived in urban boarding houses. Such places offered an almost perfectly anonymous place to live. The cities were a maze of such places, and living in one of them under an assumed name, and in a minor disguise, meant that you were difficult for law-enforcement agencies to find.

The equivalent these days is the cheap motel. Right after the bombing of the federal building in Oklahoma City, the FBI turned up several good leads from people who lived in surrounding motels. As one reporter put it, 'Such places are one step up from homelessness.' These days when you see a run-down motel, it's a fair bet that it's mostly inhabited by drifters and people on the run. The saddest thing about all this is that more and more children are being raised in these circumstances, drifting across America with their parents.

In the sunshine, the Palms looked no better than it had in the drab rainy morning of yesterday.

The same woman with the dentures and the too-vivid red hair was behind the desk again.

'You missed him this time, too,' she said.

'Missed him?'

'Paul. The night man.'

'Ah.'

She hugged her brown cardigan sweater tighter to her birdy body. 'Wish it'd warm up.'

'Do you have regulars who stay here?'

'Renters, you mean.'

'Yes. I guess that's what you'd call them.'

'They pay a special rate. They come and go,' she said. 'Sometimes we'll have quite a few of them, sometimes not.'

'You had any over the past week?'

'This about that priest?'

'Yes.'

'They're really playing it up on TV.'

I smiled. 'You noticed that, huh?'

Ever since the O. J. Simpson trial, it had become respectable for even the most staid of broadcasters to hype murders. And what could be more incendiary than a priest found murdered in a cheap motel room?

She looked at her log. 'We've got one. Tommy Hubbard.'

'A renter?'

'Yup.'

'How long's he been here?'

'Since Sunday.'

The night before the murder.

'He usually around here during the day?'

'Usually. You want his room number?'

'Please.'

She gave it to me and I said, 'You think he's around?'

'He usually is. You want me to call him?'

'That's all right.'

A call like that might warn him off. He could be gone by the time I got there.

'I appreciate the help,' I said, and walked outside.

The afternoon was heating up. Seventy-eight, according to the car radio on the way over. Looked as if spring was finally here. Maybe I'd run up and down the street in my boxer shorts or something.

As I walked down to Tommy Hubbard's room, I thought

about the incident in the restaurant a while ago. *Now* I could produce all sorts of bright and witty things to say when Bob Wilson grabbed me by the necktie. But now was a little late.

I just kept thinking about Ellie Wilson's earring in Father Daly's room.

I found the room and knocked. Behind the door, a country western singer was bleating the hell out of a sad twangy tune.

I heard a distant toilet flush. I knocked again.

I guess the name 'Tommy' had misled me into thinking that he'd be a relatively young man. He wasn't. He was white of hair, slouched of shoulder, palsied and liver-spotted of left hand. He wore a cheap jaunty red shirt and a pair of jeans low on his narrow hips. He was probably seventy. The tattoos on his knuckles were as faded as his dreams.

'Guy can't even take a dump in peace any more,' he said. 'You want something, mister?'

'My name's Payne. I'm investigating the murder of the priest the other night.'

He smiled toothlessly. His clackers were no doubt still in a glass somewhere behind him. 'I always figured those priests were grabbin' themselves a little pussy on the side. I sure as hell would.'

'Were you here the night of the murder?'

'Oh no,' he said.

' "Oh no," what?'

'No way I'm gettin' involved in this. I don't want no cops swarmin' down on me.'

'Were you here the night of the murder?'

'What if I was?'

'You might have seen something, heard something.'

'I heard what I heard and I seen what I seen.' He fixed me with a pirate's eye and said, 'You thinkin' of givin' me money?'

'I don't believe in that. You can never trust information you had to pay for. People will say anything for money.'

He cackled. 'I sure as hell will, I'll tell you that. You want me to tell you I seen a Martian, mister, you pay me enough money and I'll tell you I seen *two* Martians.'

'I'm with a law firm, by the way. Not with the police. Even if I wanted to check you out, see if you had a record or anything, I'd have a tough time doing that.'

'I didn't say I had no record.'

'Right. I only meant *if* you had a record.'

'It might be different if there was some money involved.'

'Sorry. Can't help you.'

I reached inside my suit coat, dug out a business card and handed it over to him.

'Bet these cost you a pretty penny,' he said, looking the card over.

'Not really. Just a little black type on a little white card.'

'Funny that you'd spend money for a card but not pay for information.'

'No, it isn't. The card is a legitimate business expense. Bribe money doesn't fall into that category.'

'I didn't see jackshit the other night. Or any other night.'

'All right,' I said. 'Sorry I bothered you.'

I turned and started back down the walk to my car.

From behind me, he said, 'I'll tell you what. I'll think it over.'

I just kept walking. Silently.

'Big important man,' he said, getting worked up again. 'Can't even spare a couple fucking bucks for a poor little fella like me. Big important man.'

Then his door slammed like a gunshot.

'Tommy any help to you?' the desk woman said.

'Not much, I'm afraid.'

'Kind've a strange little guy.' She laughed. 'But then you'd have to be to stay in a dump like this.'

'I'll tell the owner you said that.'

She laughed again. 'Hell, son, I *am* the owner.'

This time I laughed with her.

'If Tommy would happen to come and talk to you about the other night, would you give me a call?'

I handed out my second business card in five minutes.

'Sure,' she said. 'Be happy to.'

Then: 'But he isn't much of a talker. Not unless he's had some beer.'

'Does he drink very often?'

'Every chance he gets. I always see him in the dumpsters back there looking for cans and bottles to take back for money.'

I pulled out my wallet and laid a snappy new twenty on the counter.

'That enough to get him drunk?' I said.

'That's enough to get both of us drunk.'

'Since you're the owner, I take it you live here.'

'Got my own room, if that's what you mean. The mister and I used to live in a nice house out on Ellis Boulevard. But after he died, I just moved in here.'

'Well, why don't you treat yourself to some ice cold beer on me? And then see if Tommy has anything to tell you.'

'Be happy to.'

The twenty quickly disappeared.

'Talk to you later,' I said, and went back out into the day that was fuming with furious green spring. That's the real time machine, the way a spring day can make you feel twenty years younger. You're almost brand-new again.

ii

Bernice answered the door. She wore a different Lycra jogging suit today, but the same headband that complemented the pink hue of her suit.

'I'm looking for Jenny.'

Bernice smiled. 'Nuts. I was hoping you were looking for me.' Then, 'Some of the people are still giving us static about Jenny.'

'Static?'

She shrugged. 'She's from the halfway house nobody wanted in this neighborhood. Some of the older parish ladies are miffed at the idea of somebody like Jenny living here in the rectory. I suppose if I liked her a little better, I'd feel sorry for her.'

Bernice leaned forward. I was her confidant now. 'But between us, I worry about Jenny, too.'

'Oh?'

'A drug addict like that . . . she's liable to steal something.'

A drug addict? I thought. Jenny grew more mysterious by the minute.

But I didn't say anything to Bernice.

'I guess I thought priests took the vow of poverty,' I said, feeling inexplicably defensive about Jenny. 'I wouldn't think they'd have that much to steal.'

'Well, they have *families*, don't they? And families send them *stuff*, isn't that right?'

'I guess that's a good point.'

'So, sure they have stuff worth stealing.' Then: 'You wait here, Mr Payne. I'll go get her for you.'

'I'd appreciate that.'

Then she looked at me and said, 'Oh, dear Lord, just listen to what I've turned into.'

'Ma'am?'

'What I said about Jenny. And here I work in a rectory, too.' She shook her head. 'You know what my problem is?'

'No, I guess I don't.'

'I'm just jealous of the attention the Fathers give her. And why wouldn't they? She's an attractive young woman and I'm like an old shoe to them. Sorry I sounded off. She's actually a very decent young gal.'

After Bernice Clancy returned and escorted me to the kitchen, I watched as Jenny bent over the stove and peeked in at something in the oven.

'Be with you in a sec,' she said.

She wore stonewashed jeans that hugged her slender body lovingly. Her starchy blue man's button-down shirt gave her the same crisp air as her small no-nonsense pony tail.

'Like a cup of coffee?' she said.

'That sounds good, as a matter of fact.'

She nodded to a large window where two tall wooden stools sat. 'I like to sit there and watch the bunnies and the raccoons. They come down from the park about this time of day.'

She got us coffee and we sat and watched the bunnies and raccoons. Mid-point in the floorshow, a tiny but determined possum also showed up, figuring out a way to walk wide of the other guests, and snatch some bread for itself.

'I put out about six or seven slices a day,' she said. 'They love it.' She smiled. 'They're like my little kids.'

Her gentle voice contrasted with the pinched, hard look of her face.

She seemed to sense what I was seeing. 'I didn't sleep so good last night.'

'I didn't think sleep disorders started until you were about my age.'

'Till you're about your age or a junkie,' she said. Her lips closed tight around the word. 'The halfway house, every night people are up and walking around like zombies. I should know – I was one of them.' She nodded to me. 'I heard Bernice talking to you, again. I was a bad girl. When I heard somebody at the door, I snuck up to the front of the house. Bernice is always talking about me to somebody.'

I laughed. 'You didn't eavesdrop long enough. Bernice took back everything she said and then told me you were a nice young woman.'

'Honest to God?'

'Honest to God.'

'Well, that's sure kind of her.'

'I didn't get a chance to ask you last time. How'd you end up here? Did the priests call the halfway house?'

'I found them. I really wanted out of the halfway house, so I started looking around for some kind of job my parole counselor would approve of. What could be a better gig than a rectory, right? Father Ryan was the one who convinced the Monsignor to actually hire me. Anyway, I have a nice little room in the basement. Bernice doesn't actually live on the premises – she's got a husband and everything – so she thinks I have these special powers because I spend more time with the priests. I tried to tell her once that they depend on us both but she wouldn't listen to me.'

She stared at one of the waddling, older raccoons who was watching a golden butterfly flutter past. 'I feel kind of sorry for her. Honest. I mean, someday I'm probably going to be old and I don't want some kid like me coming in and taking over. It was the same way in the halfway house. The older junkies'd make friends with the counselors and every-thing and then they'd sort of resent it when new residents came in and hogged all the attention. You know what I'm saying?'

I nodded. 'Was Father Daly your favorite of the priests?

Since he got you in here and all?'

She'd still been staring out the window but now she turned back to me. 'Somebody told you, huh?'

'Told me?'

'About me and Father Daly.'

'No. I was watching your face when you talked about him.'

'My counselor, one thing he warned me about was getting too dependent on people, especially people I think I'm in love with. I get very possessive.'

'I'm like that, too.'

'Really? But you used to be an FBI guy.'

'What does that have to do with being possessive?'

'Well, FBI guys, so starched and everything, you know. So are you really like that – possessive?'

I smiled. '*Former* FBI guy. Not so starched and everything now. And yes, I really am like that.'

'Cool,' she said. 'Then you know what I'm talking about. I was here maybe a week and I really developed this thing for Father Daly. I couldn't help it. He was a very good-looking guy and he really knew how to handle himself around women. He'd put himself out there a little bit and then pull himself back. That really gets to me.'

'You said he "put himself out there." You mean he'd flirt with you?'

'Oh, no. It wasn't like that at all. I just meant that he'd get in these real intense conversations with you – a lot of them were about religion – and you'd think, "Hey, I'm really getting tight with this guy" and then all of a sudden he'd be really distant. And you'd feel like it was your fault or something, like you'd done or said something to offend him. You know? Off-balance, I guess you'd say. That was how I felt around him most of the time.'

'You said you were in love with him.'

'Yeah, pretty much.'

'You ever tell him that?'

Her cheeks tinted red. 'A few times, I guess.'

'What did he say?'

'Do I really have to go into this?'

'Maybe not with me, Jenny. But the police will eventually get around to asking you the same questions.'

She went back to watching the animals in the hedge-boxed back yard. The raccoons had gone over to the snake-pile of garden hose and were sniffing around that.

'He treated me like a little kid,' she said.

'So you never had a physical affair with him?'

'One night I thought we might. I mean, he took hold of my shoulders and really looked in my eyes and I got all excited but then he started shaking me.'

'Shaking you?'

'He said that I had to quit following him around all the time.'

'*Did* you follow him around all the time?'

'Yeah. Pretty much.'

'You have any idea who might have murdered him?' I said.

'I've been thinking about it.'

'And come to any conclusions?'

'Not really. He saw a lot of women in his counseling gig. Some of them developed a real thing for him.'

'Anyone in particular?'

She shrugged. 'I always noticed the way Ellie Wilson got kind of fluttery around him. You know what I'm saying? Like she couldn't stop touching him. Just little touches, but sometimes they mean a lot, right?'

'Right.'

'But I saw that in a lot of them. How they'd get real weird around him like high-school girls or something. I was the same way. I'd get real fluttery and possessive.' She shrugged. 'I'm kind of possessive myself.' Apparently she'd forgotten she'd already said that.

'Yeah?' Then: 'How did he respond to all this?'

'Oh, you could see he enjoyed it sometimes. Guess it depended on who was being fluttery.'

'Anybody else in particular comes to mind besides Ellie Wilson?'

121

'Just her. And the one who went up with him to clean out the cabin.'

'Cabin?'

She nodded and her little pony tail bounced cutely. 'Yeah. Up on the Waubeek River. Somebody who died left it to the parish a few years ago. It really needed a good cleaning-out, so Father Daly, he took this Marcia Beaumont up there and they cleaned the place up. Then he started going up there a couple of times a month. In the warm months, I mean.'

I asked her to describe where the cabin was, and she did. Vaguely.

I was going to ask her more about Marcia Beaumont but then she said, 'Are you really possessive?'

Humor the witness. 'I really am.'

She leaned forward and gave me a quick kiss on the cheek. 'Cool,' she said.

'Cool?'

'Yeah,' she laughed. 'I really like possessive people.'

'Maybe we should start a club.'

'Can I be president?' she said.

On the way out, I spoke briefly with Bernice at the front door.

'Do you think Father Daly was sleeping with anybody?'

She made a face. 'Times sure have changed when you can ask a question like that about a consecrated priest.'

'I didn't mean to upset you.'

'When I was a girl, priests were somebody you looked up to. It was almost like they were a superior race of people or something.'

Gently, I said: 'You were going to tell me about Father Daly.'

She shrugged. 'Nothing much to tell. He was a very attractive man. And being a counselor, he was in a very intimate relationship with a lot of women. But he was also very serious about being a priest. He was always praying. Always. I sensed he was having a great inner struggle. As for sleeping with women, maybe one or two, but nothing close to what the newspapers are hinting at. Nothing close to that.'

'Do you know anything about the cabin up on the Waubeek River?'

'Oh yes, the cabin. It was a little primitive for the Monsignor and Father Ryan, but Father Daly didn't mind a bit. He loved boating, so he spent quite a bit of time up there.'

'Is it locked?'

'Oh, yes. Locked tight, I think.'

'Would you have the key?'

'I think so. Yes. Are you going up there?'

'I have an old airplane I take up any chance I get. It's a nice afternoon. Might be fun to look around up there for a few hours.'

'You're as bad as Father Daly was. Any excuse to get away to the cabin and he'd be gone.'

Then she went and fetched me the key.

Half an hour later, I was at the airport.

iii

I spent five minutes checking everything over: fuel valve, engine controls, engine and flight instruments. I finished up by checking the struts and the wire that binds the wings together. Then I was getting into my leather helmet, goggles and gloves. I'd snugged on a sweater because even on a warm day, it gets chilly in an open cockpit.

I followed the river for twenty minutes and then angled eastward. Bluffs and cliffs and timbered areas contrasted with farmland. The familiar green of John Deere farm equipment was a deeper green than the land itself. A dozen horses ran in the hills above the river, and down below, on the water, a small sailing ship drifted westward.

The flight took forty minutes. I put down near a riding stables. The owner was an old friend of mine.

He must have heard me because he was in his field to watch me land, waving as I touched down.

'Wish I'd been born back then,' Sam Carson said, shaking hands as we walked toward his corral.

Sam ran the most prosperous riding academy in this part of the state. The wealthier families brought their children here to learn the ways of the saddle, as Sam liked to say.

A sign out front told just how successful he'd been:

1500 ACRES
HORSES AND SADDLES FOR SALE AND TRADE
THOROUGHBRED & PAINT & QUARTER HORSE
STUD SERVICE
HAYRIDE FACILITIES
PASTURE & STALL BOARDING FOR ALL BREEDS

Sam could never pass the sign without looking at it, a flash of pride showing in his eyes. He'd been raised by nuns in an orphanage. When I knew him at the University of Iowa, he was a shy kid in our ROTC unit. Gradually, we got to be friends and I learned just how destitute Sam was. Finishing college meant a heavy burden of student loans for him. By junior year he was working at the stables he'd eventually buy from the owner, working thirty hours a week and carrying a full load of classes. He'd graduated with a four point.

He'd had one love all the time I'd known him. Horses. He took every opportunity to be around or on a horse. I was the same way about bi-planes.

Around forty, Sam started putting on weight and his hair turned white. Not gray – white. Today he was dressed as usual – western shirt, jeans, cowboy boots, and with a pair of leather gloves tucked in his back pocket.

As we walked past the first stable, he had a word for each one of the horses. They were like his kids, though Sam and his wife had a whole tribe of the real thing up at the house.

The day smelled sweetly of hay and horseshit.

I described the cabin I was looking for and he told me the easiest way to get there. On horseback.

'You're getting the hankering, aren't you, Robert?'

'Must be,' I laughed.

'This is the third excuse in a month you've had to ride one of my horses.'

'Maybe next month I'll come up with four.'

We walked over to the smaller of two barns. A shirtless old man with muscles like a circus strongman's pounded a new shoe on the hoof of an Appaloosa saddle horse.

126

'Butch here'll be finished in a minute. How about this girl?' Sam said.

He walked over and put a big hand on the crest of the animal. Shoulder and belly and haunch were youthful and trim.

'There you go,' Butch said, setting the leg down when he was done with the hoof.

Sam led the animal into the sunlight, throwing a blanket over her as we walked.

'You want to try it this time?' Sam said.

'Think maybe I'll watch you one more time.'

Sam laughed. 'Chickenshit.' Then: 'Her name is Moonglow.'

'Moonglow?'

'Look at her forehead.'

I did, and saw what Sam was talking about. A perfect white circle of hair shone on the animal's forehead.

'Now watch closely, Robert, because next time you're going to do this yourself.'

'Yessir, bossman.'

He was probably showing off a little but he got Moonglow saddled up in under two minutes, running the skirt and fender and stirrup and cinch ring and latigo all before I even had much of a chance to see.

'You got that now?'

'Got it,' I said.

I took the reins, swung up into the saddle.

'Don't worry, Robert. You're just as impatient when you're teaching me about that old barnstormer over there.'

'Yeah, I probably am.'

'She's a good horse. You'll enjoy her. See you later. Be sure and stop up for some lemonade. Martha wants you to tell her some more FBI stories. All she reads these days is true-crime stuff. They even have pictures in some of those books. Man, times sure have changed.'

I shook my head. 'We just like to think so. But that kind of stuff has been going on ever since we started walking upright. Probably before then, even.'

He looked up at me and frowned. 'We're the only species that constantly preys on its own kind, Robert. You know that? Martha read that to me from one of her true-crime books. The only species. That's pretty depressing.'

'It sure is,' I said.

'Well, on that cheery note, Robert, have yourself a good ride.'

I nodded and rode away.

My generation got in at the tail end of the western boom. There were a few cowboy shows on TV while I was growing up but not all that many. Still, I'd had the requisite number of cowboy fantasies. In the movie theater of my mind, I was the white-hatted marshal who cleaned up the town; the spunky young man who single-handedly got rid of the vigilantes who had been terrorizing the area; and the only citizen brave enough to stand up to the gunfighter who held the town in thrall.

Those were my primary fantasies.

But there was one other. I was the scout. This was early in the 1800s. The land was still raw and vital and untouched.

This was a fantasy I still indulged in, and that's why I'd lately taken to horseback riding. Because there are places I can find today where it's possible to have a good sense of what the land looked like back then. I wanted my wife Kathy to be with me. I wanted her to see the beautiful blooming sunflowers and smell the apple blossom-breezes and watch the prairie hawks dip and dive down the air currents.

That's how I spent the first part of my ride. Trying to envision what life would have been like, back then.

Fortunately, Moonglow was a lot more sensible than I was. All the time I was playing pathfinder, she was leading us to the wooded area above the river where Father Daly's fishing cabin was located.

When we reached it, I ground-tied Moonglow and walked over to the small cabin. The house was made of pine boards, the roof of wooden shingles. Tall jack pines encircled the plot on which the cabin had been built.

There were a couple of big silver bullets in the back – propane tanks – an outdoor charcoal grill on the left side and a stack of firewood on the right.

The windows were dusty but intact. Inside, I saw that the cabin was divided into three rooms – a kind of general living area, a small bedroom with a lone single bed, and a kitchen area with an ancient refrigerator and stove. There were three cupboards, all closed. The inside looked like a doll-house for grown-ups.

I tried the door. Padlocked, just as Bernice told me it would be.

I was just inserting the key she had given me when a male voice said, 'You're trespassing, mister. Now put your hands up and turn around so I can see you.'

He was somewhere in his sixties, tall, stooped, weather-burned, and the possessor of burning blue eyes. He wore Osh-Kosh overalls, a faded checkered shirt and a long-billed blue baseball cap with a Cubs symbol on the front. He had a trusty old Remington shotgun in his gritty hands. It wasn't aimed directly at me. Not quite. But it could be. And in a matter of only moments.

He said, 'Who the hell are you, mister?'

'I'm an investigator.'

'What kind of investigator?'

'I work for a law firm.'

'What law firm?'

He would have made a good interrogation cop.

I gave him the name of the firm.

'Cedar Rapids, huh?' he said.

'Right.'

'And you're working on what, exactly?'

'There was a priest who used this cabin.'

'Yeah. I saw him around sometimes.'

'I'm trying to find out who killed him.'

'Well, then I guess we've got something in common, mister.'

The shotgun pointed downward suddenly, held in the crook of his left arm, and his right hand shot out.

We shook.

'Kevin Ward's my name.'

'Robert Payne.'

'Just wanted to make sure who you were,' he said. 'I figure with all the publicity, lot of people around here'll come in and scavenge the cabin.'

'It's locked.'

'They'll break in.'

'Doesn't look like there's much of any value inside.'

'That's not the point. People who scavenge, most of them do it for the thrill, not the loot.'

'I guess you're probably right about that.' I turned toward the door. 'You want to come in with me?'

He nodded and followed me inside.

The air smelled of fireplace wood and mildew. These old cabins were never water-tight.

'You looking for anything in particular, mister?'

'Nope. Don't have any idea of what I'm looking for actually.'

I started going through the cupboards.

'He was a nice fella,' Kevin Ward said. 'Didn't think I'd like him at first. He was pretty modern.'

Modern obviously being a word that conveyed a whole load of negatives to Kevin Ward.

'But one day I was explainin' to him about this grandson of mine my daughter was havin' trouble with, and Father Daly told me a few things to tell Bonnie, you know, to help her boy and everything, and damned if they didn't help. They really did. Always be grateful to the man for that. I sure will. I'm not even no Catholic.'

Nothing of note in the kitchen. Father Daly obviously ate out of cans up here. Probably caught a few fish, cleaned them, cooked them on that grill out there, and then filled in with the cans of baked beans and beets and green beans in the cupboard.

Nothing in the bedroom area. The bed was neatly made with a faded and ragged old comforter on top.

In the living-room area, I picked up all the cushions on the spavined couch, and looked down below for anything that might have fallen down there.

'You live nearby?' I asked.

'Yeah. Quarter of a mile is all. Little farm up to the west there. Plant some corn and soybeans. Raise a few head of cattle. Pretty small-time.'

'Did Father Daly ever seem . . . troubled or anything?'

Kevin Ward shrugged. 'Lots of times. He was one of those fellas who thinks too much. You could see it in his face most of the time. You could be standin' right next to him but he was really off somewheres else. You know what I mean?'

'Right. You ever hear any arguments or anything?'

He looked surprised. 'Yeah. Matter of fact, about a week ago I heard one. Father Daly was really mad at somebody. I was walkin' up the path over there. Didn't come close enough to the cabin to see who it was he was talkin' to, but he just kept sayin' "This is insane. This is really insane. Don't you know that? Don't you realize what you're doing?" '

'The other person didn't speak?'

'Not so's I could hear, anyway.'

'Could it have been a woman?'

'Coulda been. Sorry I can't help you more, mister.'

I looked around the living room. I'd left one of the couch cushions at an angle.

When I walked over to straighten it out, I accidentally knocked a couple of magazines off the arm of the couch.

When they hit the floor, the magazines fell open.

In the center of one of them was a newspaper clipping. I bent over and picked it up.

LOCAL MAN MURDERED

Michael James Grady, 34, was found dead Tuesday night near the picnic grounds where his bowling team was

having its annual picnic. At press time, a police spokesman refused to comment on the details of Grady's death.
Hospital sources, however, revealed that Grady had suf-
fered multiple stab wounds and that both ears had been
severed.

The rest of the story talked about the pending inquest,
Grady's military service and his family and the various
organizations he belonged to. Then I found more newspaper
cuttings. They referred to the equally grisly deaths of two
other men – Lawrence Lynnward and Frank Mason. The
murders had taken place several months apart.

'Find something?'

I put the clipping in my shirt-pocket. 'I'm not sure.'

'Hope you get something for coming out here. It's a long
ways from Cedar Rapids.'

'Actually, I'm enjoying myself.' I told him about my
bi-plane and the horse.

'You know Sam Carson, huh?'

'Sure do.' In case he was about to say something negative, I
said, 'He's one of my best friends.'

'Great guy. The missus and I always go on his hayrack
rides in the fall. Have ourselves a wonderful time.'

I looked around the cabin. If there was anything more to
find, it would take a better detective than me to unearth it.

'You flyin' back?' Kevin Ward said as I locked up the cabin.
'Sure am.'

'Why'n't you fly over my farm? The missus and I'll be
watching for you.'

He looked and sounded like a kid. That's the best part of us
all, I sometimes think. That ten per cent of us that never
grows up, but which somehow remains, despite all the sorrow and cynicism of the world, essentially innocent.

'I'll do better than that for you,' I said. 'I'll buzz your
farmhouse two or three times.'

He grinned. 'The missus loves stuff like that. Just loves it.'

He walked me back up the path to where I'd ground-tied

Moonglow, watched me swing myself up into the saddle, and then said he'd see me in a little while when I buzzed his house.

I took Moonglow the long way back, and savored every minute of it.

I guess the first thing I noticed about Sunset Towers was that it didn't *have* any towers. Oh well.

The nursing home was designed to resemble a pricy hotel of four stories, with an outdoor swimming pool, two tennis courts and a practice range for golf.

'We're like a family here,' said the funereal young man in the blue suit.

I noticed, however, that as we passed up and down the halls looking at sleeping arrangements, showers and dining facilities, not one of the residents acknowledged him in any way. In fact, they looked a little wary of him.

The place did not smell of fecal matter, none of the residents wore any black eyes or bruises, nor did I hear the screams of an elderly woman being raped.

The food was probably bland, the staffers were probably given to impatience and even surliness on occasion, and my friend Eugene here in the blue suit was probably a past master of subtle intimidation.

But all in all, the place was squeaky clean and bright, and the residents looked reasonably content.

We spent twenty minutes discussing financial arrangements. My mother had left me some insurance money that I'd invested. It would take all that and some more to put Vic up here for his final months but I was willing to do it.

I sure as hell didn't want to live with him.

Eugene gave me several brochures and a long piece of paper listing all the things Vic would need to bring with him.

On the way out, I saw a sweet little old woman standing by one of the windows, gazing out.

I thought I'd ask her how she liked it here. But when I

spoke, she said nothing, just looked at me with sad, ancient and very moist eyes.

I tried hard to convince myself that her moist eyes had nothing to do with conditions here at Sunset Towers.

'You're really going to put him in a home?' Felice said after we were in bed later on. I had my western novel and jammies. She had her Dean Koontz novel and jammies.

'It's what he needs.'

'Maybe it is. But not in these circumstances.'

'You're really mad, aren't you?'

'Damned right, I am.'

'I'm trying to do the right thing, Felice, whether you think so or not.'

'You know something, Robert?'

'What?'

'Right now I don't like you very much.'

'Well, right now I don't like you very much, either.'

'Tough titty,' she said and rolled over on her side and began reading.

But I was too upset to read. I said, 'You're always taking *his* side, Felice. The same way my mother did.'

She looked over at me. Her eyes glistened with tears. 'He's dying and he's all alone, Robert. And you don't seem to give a damn at all.'

And with that, she shut off her reading light and slipped on her sleep mask.

iv

I spent two hours that afternoon at the law offices trying to persuade the key witness in our vehicular homicide trial to testify. Her name was Beverly Wright and she was having some second thoughts. She was going to be in the news a lot and that frightened her. The reporters would try to make her look like a bad person and a liar – as if she were fabricating her story.

Brad Doucette talked to her for a while, got frustrated, sent me in as kind of the second team, and when I didn't seem to be getting anywhere, put himself back in the game. He spent nearly a half an hour with Ms Wright and still got nowhere, so then it was back to me.

I couldn't honestly blame her. Prosecuting attorneys are very skilled at making unfriendly witnesses look stupid and venal. The press, too, especially in its ambush journalism mode, can easily do the same.

All you have to do is walk to your car with a number of reporters trailing you and firing questions, and the public just assumes you're hiding something.

But without her testimony, our client had very little chance of proving his innocence. Was our client an arrogant, pushy, self-absorbed bastard? You bet. But, in this case anyway, I believed he was innocent.

'My folks just don't want me to get involved,' Beverly told me. 'Neither does my son. He's fourteen. He likes Aaron a lot.

My son's one of the few people Aaron's nice to. But he still doesn't want me to get involved. Because of the, you know, the publicity. I mean, you know what they're going to call me when they get me up on that stand.'

'What're they going to call you?'

'A whore. Right?'

How could I disagree? They might use a cleverer word than that to convey their meaning, but the meaning would be the same nonetheless.

Aaron Grant was a local manufacturer. He was also a prominent Republican, having served as State Chair a few times. He was also married and the father of three, and a lay minister at his church. He was noted for his angry sermons on family values.

Beverly Wright was a member of the same church. She was divorced, with the one son.

Aaron and Beverly had had a thing going for nearly a year now. Aaron went through one of those idiotic transformations middle-aged men sometimes do. This stalwart Republican and family-values man started wearing his graying hair in a tiny pony tail, driving around in a Mercedes sports coupé, and spending a lot of time and money on the riverboat casinos up on the Mississippi.

He was also hopping into bed with Beverly whenever he got the chance.

One more thing about Aaron: while he wasn't an alcoholic, his taste for alcohol had certainly increased this past year. He'd even taken to having a few drinks at lunch, something he'd always frowned upon, both for himself and his employees.

The trouble started with alcohol.

One night, after getting back from the riverboat, Aaron was driving down a dark street when a man suddenly appeared in his headlights. Aaron's car struck the man. Aaron's car killed the man.

An interesting fact: the dead man's blood alcohol content was even higher than Aaron's.

The incident became a scandal – couldn't help but be, given

Aaron's standing in the community. Aaron insisted that he had not been speeding, that the man had simply wandered directly into the path of his car.

Here was the part that gave me my first inkling of respect for Aaron: even though he knew that Beverly's testimony as to how much he'd drunk that night could probably save him, he didn't press her to appear in court for him.

Some of his family-values sermons had apparently rubbed off. Aaron was going to save Beverly's family – not to mention his own family – from scandal.

Brad Doucette knew better, of course. Aaron was the kind of guy juries sometimes liked to hang. Too much money. Too much loose living.

He needed a witness, and badly. He needed Beverly.

'We've still got three days before the trial, Beverly,' I said. 'Will you at least please think it over?'

She was a pretty woman rather than a beauty but with great dignity and poise.

'Are you kidding?' she said. 'It's all I *do* think about.' Then: 'How's Aaron?'

Everybody involved had decided that it would be better if Aaron and Beverly no longer saw each other. So they both asked us frequently for reports on the other person. I felt sorry for Aaron's wife and family, for Beverly and her son, and even for Aaron to some degree. Nobody involved was really a bad person.

She stood up, trim in her white ruffled blouse and blue skirt.

She put out a hand and we shook.

'You're nice,' she said. 'I appreciate that. Your colleague Brad's a little pushy for my taste.'

I smiled. 'Brad? Pushy? I don't think I've ever heard anybody say that before.'

I spent the hour after that going through some of my notes about Father Daly. I also added the other newspaper clippings to the file.

Why had Father Daly collected clippings about unsolved murders that had taken place in the past few years? And who was he arguing with at the fishing cabin that night?

The receptionist buzzed me and I picked up.

Gilhooley said, 'Thought I'd check in with you.'

'I was wondering what was going on.'

'I've just been doing my character sketches.'

That's what Gilhooley calls the reports he gives me, and that's what they sometimes read like. He supplies me with a one-page description of a person's life. Everything is there – family, education, employment, penchants – writ bold and large.

'Anything interesting?'

'Not much. Gray and Ryan served together in a small town called Holbrook right after getting out of seminary.'

'By any chance was Father Daly there, too?'

'No. He first served in a place up near Dubuque. Same diocese, though.'

'You were checking out the rectory staff, too.'

'Right. Bernice Clancy, zilch. Raised four children. Husband has Parkinson's. Worked as a teacher's assistant at St Mallory's grade school for eleven years then switched to the rectory and became the housekeeper.'

'And Jenny?'

'Bingo.'

'Jenny is bingo?'

'Junkie for one thing.'

'Right.'

'Fourteen months at Mitchellville for shoplifting and violating parole. Then she went to a halfway house in Cedar Rapids.'

'I pretty much knew that.'

'You know about the counselor at the halfway house?'

'I guess not.'

'Here's where I earned my money, Robert. Jenny is one of these chicks who really get hung up on certain people. She developed an obsession for this counselor named Jim Robbins and just wouldn't let go of it. She even called Robbins' wife a few times and hinted that the guy was gonna leave his family and run off with her – Jenny, I mean.'

'Right.'

'According to the people who knew your Father Daly, Jenny developed the same kind of infatuation with him. She was really dependent – constantly following him around and telling him that they should be together.'

Are you really possessive?

'And you want to know the zinger?' Gilhooley said.

'The zinger?'

'I talked to somebody at the halfway house, and guess what? Robbins wouldn't press charges. That's the only thing that kept Jenny from going to the slam.'

'Why should she go to the slam?'

'Listen to this. One night when he was in his office, she snuck in and tried to stab him with a butcher knife.'

4:

POLICE DEPARTMENT

Ronald Dayne Swanson
Age: 56
Race: Caucasian
Occupation: Insurance Company
Executive
Marital Status: M
Military Service: 6 years USAF,
1961-1967

Swanson: It's something that people get very
angry about. And it's just so irrational
when you look back in history . . .
particularly to the Greeks. As much
as it seems to sicken people in our
society . . . there were a lot of
instances of adults and children
having sexual liaisons. A lot of the
most prominent Greeks – and later
Romans – did this quite openly. I see
this as being very beneficial for the
child . . . he begins having adult
insights into the world that he
couldn't have otherwise. And the
Internet, of course, has made this all
the more fun: it's like ordering from
a menu . . . all the photos and

videotape. I believe that when our
world becomes truly civilized, we'll
take the same attitude toward it that
the Greeks and Romans had.

Ronald Swanson

A nice, sweet little black one.

That's who he is after today.

He's wearing his disguise as usual. The red baseball cap, the thick horn-rimmed glasses. And the limp. That's the master-stroke.

If anybody reports him to the police, that's what they'll remember most. The limp.

Pretty damned good, he thinks. He's only fifteen years old and he's already thinking on the genius level.

The nice, sweet little black one is sitting under a tree on the small hill overlooking the swimming pool below.

Hot August afternoon like this one, the pool is packed with screaming, laughing kids. A feast for somebody like him.

The thing is, you have to be very, very selective in choosing the right one.

The thing is, you have to be very, very careful in how you approach her.

The thing is, sometimes the cops are the least of your worries. You run into a father or an older brother, you'd wish the cops *had* caught you.

Guys like him get killed all the time.

But of course, that's part of the fun, isn't it?

The danger of it all . . .

That's when he thinks of the double ice-cream gambit.

It worked for him last week. Sweet little blonde girl. Age

seven. And when he was through with her in the woods, he let her go. Safe and sound. No harm done.

Yes, the double ice-cream gambit.

He limps over to the concession stand, which is packed with kids, most of whom are at least partly naked, the boys just in swim trunks, the girls in skimpy swim suits.

Takes him ten minutes to work his way up in line.

'Two ice-cream cones. Vanilla.'

'Two scoops or one?'

He pauses. Why not shoot for the moon? If one scoop snagged the little blonde girl last week, then two scoops now is certain to double his luck.

'Two scoops.'

The thing is, it's so hot today that by the time he's starting to walk up the hill to the little black girl, the ice-cream is already melting.

All over his hands.

Sticky. Which means flies . . .

The little girl sits under the tree in her pink one-piece bathing suit watching the white boy approach her.

Next to her is the white towel she dried off with after the pool, and inside the towel are the two tokens her mom gave her for the bus ride home. Her mom also gave her two one dollar bills but those were spent on the Power Rangers comic she just finished reading, and on the Baby Ruth bar she just finished eating . . .

The funny thing is, the white boy is walking right toward her.

She thought he was probably just going up over the hill to where the bus seats were.

But, no.

He's looking right at her . . .

And he's walking right toward her . . .

White people in general scare her – white folks put both her dad and her older brother in jail – but this one doesn't scare her for some reason . . .

The limp, she decides.

That's why he doesn't scare her.

She's learned that people with arms missing or bad legs or faces burned ... they generally treat little black girls a lot nicer. Because people don't like them much better than they like black people ...

She almost smiles when she sees how the two ice-cream cones are melting all over his hands.

Kind of a dorky kid, like her little brother Leon.

Dorky but sweet.

When he reaches her, he says, 'Hi.'

'Hi.'

'You seen a red-haired boy around?'

'A red-haired boy?'

'Uh-huh.'

'Huh-uh. Guess I haven't.'

'Darn.'

'What's wrong?'

'He must've taken the bus home without me. He forgets things sometimes. He got his head injured in a car accident and he hasn't been quite right since.'

'Oh.'

'I got this butter brickle ice-cream cone for him.' Then, 'You like butter brickle?'

'Sure.'

'Why don't you take it, then?'

'Me?'

'It's melting. You might as well. Otherwise, I'll just have to throw it away. I can't eat two of them all by myself.'

'Well.'

Fir the first time, he sees suspicion in her eyes.

He smiles. 'Your mom told you not to, huh?'

'Told me not to?'

'Take stuff from strangers.'

The girl looks embarrassed, then, as if he's read her mind or something. 'Yeah. Yeah, she did.'

'How old are you?'

'Eleven.'

Couple years older than she looks. He doesn't actually like them this old. Not usually.

'Well, then you're old enough to tell good people from bad people, aren't you?'

She shrugs. 'Maybe, I guess.'

'Do I look like a bad person?'

She squints up at him in the sunlight. 'I guess not.'

Even up here, you can smell the chlorine from the pool below. The cry of children is loon-loud.

He puts out his hand. 'It's melting fast.'

'Well,' she says, her eyes filling with the cone.

'Two dips,' he says. 'Nice and cold for a hot day.'

He pushes the cone toward her a few more inches.

'Doesn't it look good?'

'Uh-huh,' she says.

'Then you better take it.'

'Well,' she says.

And takes it.

He gives her a few minutes to enjoy her cone.

He stands above her, looking around for any sign of cops or park rangers. Bastards are everywhere these days.

'How's it taste?'

She grins. 'Great.'

He watches the way she licks her cone, little pink tongue working.

'You like ducks?'

'You mean quack-quack ducks?'

He laughs. 'Yes, quack-quack ducks.'

'They're cute, I guess.'

'You know where the duck pond is over there?'

He points to an area of forest about a city block away.

'I went there once when I was a little girl,' she says.

'They're a lot of fun to watch. You know, swimming around and everything. Why don't we go there now?'

'Well.'

'Your mom again, huh?'

'She said I shouldn't ever go anywhere with strangers.'

'Gosh, I thought we were friends.'

'Well.'

'Guess I thought when you took the ice-cream cone, that meant we were friends. And trusted each other.'

He's honed this particular melodrama down to a fine point. Little kids always go for his hurt-feelings speech. They get eager to make him feel better . . . and then they'll do what he says.

'Guess I knew you couldn't trust me . . .' he says.

Then he notices her gaze.

Still squinting into the sun, she is, but no longer squinting at him.

But at something behind him.

He turns to see what she's staring at and –

—oh, my God.

He's at least six feet and 200 pounds and even from here he can feel the black man's ire.

'Who's that?'

'My brother Bobby. He just got out of jail for whupping his girlfriend's old boyfriend. Put him in the hospital.'

'Oh, shit.'

'Here,' he says. 'Why don't you take my cone, too?'

'Don't you want to meet Bobby?'

Panic. He can just imagine what this guy'll do him.

'Here.'

And thrusts his own melting cone into her hand.

And then he starts walking away fast up the hill. Forget the limp. Forget the disguise.

When he crests the hill, he risks his first look-back.

The little girl is standing up and talking to her brother.

She's pointing up the hill.

Oh, God. What if her brother comes after him?

He runs the half block to where a bus is parked.

He doesn't even give a damn where the bus is going. He'll catch the right one later on.

He swings up on the steep bus step and drops his money in the coin box.

Then the bus moves away from the curb and starts to take off.

Which is when the little girl and her brother appear at the top of the hill.

The brother looks angry, glaring around for sight of the kid who was fooling with his little sister.

Faster, faster he mentally urges the bus driver. God, can't this thing go faster?

He doesn't relax until he's downtown and changing on to the bus that will take him out to his nice white suburb.

So close this time.

Came so close to getting caught.

He shudders and then looks over at the old lady who's watching him.

He stares out the window.

So damned close this time.

Four

i

Just before five o'clock, my phone rang. The receptionist said, 'There's a man on line four for you.'

'A man?'

'I'm sorry, Robert. He wouldn't give me his name.'

'Thanks, Doris.'

I picked up.

'Payne?'

'Yes.'

'This is Tommy.'

He sounded pissed. 'Yeah, Tommy. From the mo-tel. The Palms.'

'Oh, right. What can I do for you, Tommy?'

'You know those gift books the Grant Cafeterias give out?'

Grant Cafeterias were a big Midwestern chain. Good food, though of the old style, lots of heavy gravy and sugar-coating.

'You bring me one of them gift books, and I'll tell you something you'll want to hear.'

'Giving you money would be a bribe, but this—'

'—is just a gift.'

'Right,' I said. I smiled to myself. Circumstances or fate had forced Tommy to scuttle across the floor of our silent social seas. He'd learned how to be shrewd.

'So I give you a gift book and—'

151

'—I give you information. It's called barter.'

'Yeah, I guess that *is* what it's called, isn't it?'

'I'll be here for another hour and a half, you want to come over.'

There was a Grant's on the same side of town as the Palms Motel so I stopped there. They had two gift book prices, $25 and $50. Grant's didn't sell booze, so Hubbard wasn't going to drink it up. And they didn't sell drugs, so he wasn't going to drug it up. And you could purchase the kind of gift book that you couldn't hand in for cash. He was going to have a few healthy meals. I bought him the $50 book.

The voices of newscasters drifted from every open motel window. Meal-time. Battered cars and battered people hunkered down for whatever repast the begrudging gods had laid on for them, this particular evening.

Late afternoon sunlight cast the Palms into long, deep shadows that actually made the place look a lot better.

I knocked on Tommy's door less than half an hour after he'd called.

The clothes were probably Salvation Army but it was the intent of them that moved me. He was all dressed up, Tommy was. Sport coat, slacks, white shirt, necktie. That all these clothes were a few eras out of date didn't matter. Nor did their slightly rumpled condition.

Tommy was all dressed up and he was going to take his Grant's gift book and have himself a good meal.

'Here you go,' I said, and handed him the certificate book. We were having our usual meeting in his doorway. Apparently, Tommy had never heard of inviting people into your room.

He fanned the certificates the way he would have fanned a wad of money.

'You got the fifty-dollar one,' he said. 'That's damned nice of you.'

I get sentimental. I can't help it. Poor old bastard struggling along and barely making it and then a bit of luck falls into his hands. It's nice to think there are at least a few happy endings in this life of ours.

'So,' I said, 'you're all dressed up to go and use your Grant's certificate book, huh?'

'This, you mean?' he said, pointing with his right hand to the book in his left.

'Yeah.'

'Nah. I'll save this for a special occasion. I've got a meeting to go to right now.'

'Oh yeah, a meeting?'

'Yeah. I belong to the Midnight Rangers.'

I saw the humor in it but somehow I didn't feel like laughing. Here I'd been thinking I was helping some nice old guy out with some food certificates, but—

But.

The Midnight Rangers were one of the new fascist groups we're getting out here on the prairies. They hate, in no special order, Jews, blacks, gays, feminists, and liberals of all stripes. Their local heroes are two guys who doused a black man with gasoline and then set him on fire. Despite a lot of evidence to the contrary – including the victim's identification of the two men – the Rangers insist that their buddies were framed by the Jews.

Tommy smirked. 'Take it you don't like the Rangers, huh?'

'Most of them are just thugs and grifters.'

The eyes sparkled with malice. 'Well, you better get used to us because we're gonna be here for a long time. The white man needs to take his country back.'

I wanted to punch the bastard. And then I wanted to punch myself for being so naive about people.

Nice old man.

A good solid Midwestern meal in his good solid Midwestern belly.

And then he turns out to be a creep of the worst kind.

'So what did you want to tell me?' I said.

'About the guy I seen leaving his room the other night.'

'His being—'

'—that priest who got killed. I seen him on TV this afternoon.'

'The priest?'

'No, the guy.'

'The one leaving his room?'

'Yeah.'

'Can you describe him?'

'Hell, I can give you his name.'

'Really?'

'Yep. Bob Wilson. He was on the news with this other priest. I saw you talking to him yesterday when you first came out here.'

'Other priest? Monsignor Gray?'

'Right. Monsignor Gray. This Wilson guy was with him on television. And he was here that night.'

'You're absolutely sure it was Wilson?'

'Absolutely.'

I thought of my conversation with Ellie Wilson. I'd had the sense that there was a lot she hadn't told me.

Now Tommy here had put her husband in Father Daly's motel room.

'You'd be willing to tell the police this?'

He shook his head. 'No way. No cops. That'd bring those bastards down on the Rangers and I wouldn't want to do it to those boys. They're my friends.'

'How did you happen to see Wilson leaving Father Daly's room? It was pretty late.'

'Can't sleep lately. We're talking about buying an old house and fixing it up so the Rangers can have a kind of permanent place.'

'I don't understand what that has to do with your being up so late.'

'Excitement. I was just smokin' a cigarette in the doorway here, the way I sometimes do when I want to get a breeze, and I seen this man leavin' the room.'

'He see you?'

'Don't think so. He went the opposite direction.'

'And you don't have any doubts it was Wilson?'

'No doubts at all.'

He tapped the gift book.

'If I didn't have that Rangers meeting, I'd go right to Grant's now and have me some of their pecan pie. You ever have their pecan pie?'

'Guess not.'

'Great stuff.' Then: 'You shoulda seen your face when I told you I was a Ranger. That's how most people look when they find out.'

He snorted and grinned. 'They hate our guts, all those niggers and fags and kikes, and we like it just fine.'

He wanted to rile me but I wasn't going to give him the pleasure.

'You take care of yourself now, Mr Payne,' he said, his voice exultant. He was a canny old bastard and he figured he'd just put one over on the rube who'd given him the food certificate book.

The hell of it was, he *had* just put one over on me. Sometimes I really *was* a rube, the proverbial small-town Iowan. It's just part of my nature by now, I guess.

I started across town but then stopped and turned. I just kept seeing Felice's face. I'd never seen her this angry or disappointed in me.

When I opened up my apartment door, I stepped into a very dark room. The only light came from far down the hall near the bathroom.

As I drew closer, I heard Vic say, 'I can't say he's wrong, Felice. His dad was a real good guy. Played baseball with him and took him camping and fishing all the time. You know, stuff like that.'

'We're not all alike, Vic. It wasn't your fault you weren't the outdoorsy type.'

'Oh hell, Felice, I wasn't any kind of a father to him at all. All I ever did was hang around the house and drink martinis with my drunken advertising friends. He really hated them, Robert did, and I suppose they were pretty bad people. Mostly drunks, I guess.'

By now, I was at the door to the room and could see what was going on.

Vic was packing his suitcase.

He saw me before she did. 'Hey, Robert, how's it going?'

This was the hearty, social Vic. Or that's what he was trying to be. He didn't sound real hearty or social at the moment.

'Hi, Felice,' I said.

She looked at me but didn't speak. The rage was gone from her eyes but now there was just a sorrow that was a whole lot worse to see.

'Packing up, huh?' I said stupidly.

'Yep. Packing up,' Vic said. 'That nursing home of yours has a waiting list a mile long, but I found another place. A hospice. They said they could take me the day after tomorrow.'

'I hope it's a nice place, Vic,' I said, speaking more gently to him than I probably ever had before.

'Yeah. I made a couple of calls tonight,' he said, dropping a pair of balled-up socks in the open suitcase on the bed. 'Asked a few of my friends what they thought of the place. They said it was real nice, and that I was real lucky.'

He was coiling up a belt when he stopped suddenly and said, 'You think I could talk to you a minute, Robert?'

I looked at Felice. 'Uh, sure, Vic.'

'I'd appreciate it.'

She leaned forward and kissed him on the cheek and then walked out of the room. She didn't once glance at me. She closed the door behind her.

He stood by the open suitcase and said, 'I'm not worth a damn at saying stuff like this.'

He looked at me directly. 'I just want to thank you, Robert.'

Thank me? I thought. *I'm throwing you out and you're thanking me?*

'I know this is going to take a lot of money, you putting me in the home and everything and I just wanted to say—'

Then he choked up, shaky tears in his voice and eyes, and then he started hacking.

'Just give me a minute,' he said between coughing spells.

I wanted to feel sorry for him but I couldn't. Every time I saw him I was fifteen years old again, and he was stealing my mother from me, and dishonoring my father's name. Vic and Mom, Mom and Vic, it was as if my dad had never existed. Mom and Vic, Vic and Mom, always hanging out with those advertising people, and rushing off to parties and awards banquets and more parties. Mom and Vic, Vic and Mom.

Finally, the coughing got so bad that he had to sit down on the edge of the bed.

When the spasm was over, he said, 'I hope you don't hate me as much as you used to.'

'Oh hell, Vic, listen—'

He held up a hand. 'I want to tell you one thing before I start coughing again, Robert.'

He was panting now, breathless, but he gathered himself and said, 'Your mother was the love of my life. She really was. But I always knew that she'd never love me as much as she had your father. I guess that's why I always tried to make sure that we had plenty of booze and parties and noisy friends in our life. So she wouldn't have time to realize that I could never live up to your father's memory.'

'Look, Vic—'

He held up his hand again, started to cough, swallowed it down. 'And in the process of keeping your mother busy all the time, I fell down on the job of being your stepfather. I didn't pay any attention to you and I realize now how wrong that was.' The tears were back in his eyes and voice again. 'I always thought you were a pretty good kid, Robert.'

He started crying then, an old dying man, a man that I'd happened to know for all but fourteen years of my life, an utter stranger.

'Thanks for paying for the hospice, Robert,' he said, trying to snuffle up his tears and dry his eyes. 'I can't tell you how much I appreciate it.'

'You don't owe me any thanks, Vic. You really don't.' I

made a show of glancing at my wrist-watch. 'Guess I need to get back at it.'

Some more snuffling, and he said: 'You're a damned good man, Robert. You really are.' Then: 'You know what you could do for me sometime?'

'What's that?'

'Take me up in that bi-plane of yours.'

She was in the kitchen making two cups of de-caf tea.

I came up behind her, took her slender shoulders, but she shrugged me off.

'For what it's worth,' I said, 'we had a very nice talk in there. Probably the best talk we've ever had in our lives. He's very grateful that I'm paying for the hospice.'

She carried the whistling kettle over to the two cups she'd set out on the counter.

'It's not an act of generosity,' she said. 'It's an act of selfishness.'

'I'm really not up for this shit.'

'Well, I guess I'm really not up for your shit either, Robert.' She fixed me with her lovely blue eyes. 'You're not who I thought you were, I guess.'

'I'm going now.'

'Good.'

'I don't have to justify myself to him. Or you, for that matter.'

'You're right,' she said. 'You don't need to justify yourself to either of us.'

'I didn't ask him to come here.'

'I realize that, Robert.'

She set about putting lemon slices and sugar cubes on the saucers.

'I just want to say one thing to you, one thing I've learned for myself.'

'All right.' I tried to sound like I was real interested.

'You're never going to be an adult, Robert, until you've accepted him and forgiven him. He's not a perfect human

158

being but neither are you. He did love your mother. And even you've told me that he took very good care of her. And he understood that he would always be second-best in her eyes, and he accepted that and made his peace with it. He probably was a bad stepfather, but were you the perfect stepson? You were so wrapped up in your anger over your father that you didn't even try to accept him. So you weren't perfect, either, Robert. You weren't perfect, either.'

She had the cups of tea ready to go.

'I just want you to think about that, Robert.'

I felt confused and lonely, and terribly sorry for myself.

I tried to kiss her but she moved away just in time to avoid me.

'I'd better get these in there before they get cold,' she said.

ii

The Wilsons lived in an expensive area of the city, in a formidable house of glass and brick with strong linear roof lines and three balconies. By now, I had my headlights on and all the time I was angling my way up the steep curving asphalt drive, I sensed eyes upon me. Probably somebody peering out from one of those wide but cunningly concealed balconies.

A new Mercedes Benz four-door sedan and a two-door BMW were parked outside the attached three-stall garage.

Twilight had turned the sky a purple color that I always associate with the Nevada desert. Birds cried intense and lonely songs in the hardwood windbreak on the west side of the house.

As I walked up to the door, I breathed in some of the expensive air. It smelled and tasted fresh.

Ellie Wilson opened the door. 'Mr Payne. I'm surprised to see you.'

'I'd like to talk to Bob, if that's possible.'

'Why, of course. But it probably would've been better if you'd called ahead. He's on the phone long-distance with his brother right now. Sometimes they talk for more than an hour. One time they talked two hours.'

If she was nervous about me meeting Bob, she hid it well. She was dressed in a tailored black and white houndstooth suit. Her blonde hair was swept back into a loose chignon. The effect of the hairstyle emphasized her long and elegant neck, and the fine classical bones of her face. The suit made me wonder if she was just getting in, or going out.

'Why don't I get you something to drink,' she said, 'and then I'll let Bob know you're here.'

She stood back to let me into the house. 'I should apologize for the scene at the restaurant.'

'Thank you – but it really wasn't your fault.'

'Are you here to talk more about Father Daly?'

'Yes.'

'I just hope we can get this wrapped up soon. It's already hurting the fund-raising, according to Bob. He had lunch at his country club this afternoon and several of the men there said they'd rather hold the checks they pledged. They want to see where this all leads.'

'Where it leads?'

'You know, if there is some kind of scandal involved.'

I shrugged. 'A priest being found murdered in a motel room is already something of a scandal, I'd think.'

We talked as she guided me through the house. The foyer led to a step-down living room with a dramatic sloped ceiling, a huge fireplace and three sliding glass doors. The air was even more expensive inside than it had been outside.

I sat in a leather armchair near the darkened fireplace.

'A beer for you, or a drink?'

'Diet Pepsi if you've got it.'

She laughed. 'Don't let my husband hear you say that. He doesn't trust people who don't drink. He says that they have something to hide and that they're afraid it'll come out.'

'I'll still take a Diet Pepsi.'

Losing points with Bob Wilson didn't exactly intimidate me.

She started to walk away and I said, 'You never did explain how your earring got in Father Daly's room the other night.'

'No,' she said, looking at me bluntly. 'I guess I never did, did I?'

She turned and walked out of the room.

I felt self-conscious sitting in the armchair so I got up and walked around. The sunken living room was like a gladiatorial pit, the weapons of choice being the innuendo and insult and smirk favored by the country clubbers Ellie had mentioned earlier. Their weapons were every bit as deadly as the spears and knives and hand-axes favored by the Roman gladiators.

There was an antique table in one corner, covered with family photographs.

There were five Wilsons: Bob, Ellie and two girls and a boy. The kids all looked healthy and sane. Bob managed to swagger even while he was standing still to pose. All of Ellie's photos depicted a woman with a distinct air of melancholy about her. The most intriguing photo showed a sweet-faced Ellie at age five or six, two of her front teeth gone, being held up in the arms of a slight, handsome man in a DX service station uniform.

'That's my father,' she said from behind me, 'on the happiest day of his life. He came back from the Korean War with a badly fractured leg and nightmares about how he'd been tortured as a prisoner of war. He hadn't finished high school so his options were limited. He spent fifteen years working in gas stations owned by other people. Then on his fortieth birthday, he opened his own station. That's the photo you're looking at.'

'Even back then you looked a little sad.'

I set the picture down, turned around, and accepted the glass of Diet Pepsi she handed me.

'I didn't care much for my mother,' Ellie said. 'She went out a lot on my father, and it eventually broke him. Spiritually, I mean. He was always sure she would change someday but she never did. I guess some of his sadness rubbed off on me.'

That didn't fit in with what I'd been told about Ellie's mother being super-religious. Or maybe it did. Maybe she'd punished Ellie so harshly to assuage her own guilt. And maybe Ellie had done the same to her children.

None of this was anything I could ask about.

'Just what we need,' Bob Wilson said. 'More psycho-babble. Didn't you get enough of that with Father Daly?'

He'd obviously been listening. He was also obviously unhappy.

He wore a white button-down shirt, V-neck brown sweater, tan chinos and white running shoes. He carried a drink the color of honey. Scotch, I assumed.

'Ellie loves drama,' he said. 'She can never get enough of it, can you, dear?'

'Just the way you can never get enough of bimbos, I suppose.'

He laughed. 'We're giving you a taste of our home-life, Payne. But believe me, it can get a lot rougher than this.' He went up and put a fond arm on Ellie's slender shoulders. 'I need women in my life, and she needs grief. We're a perfect match.'

'I'll leave you two alone,' she said, sliding out from his heavy arm. 'I'll talk to you later, Robert.'

When she was gone, he said, 'The first thing I want to do is apologize for the scene I made in the restaurant. I'm a total ass sometimes. You want some scotch?'

'No, thanks.'

'Let's sit down.'

We sat in facing leather armchairs and he said, 'You don't have anything in mind where my wife's concerned, do you?'

'You mean like sex?'

'I mean exactly like sex.'

'She's a beautiful woman.'

'And that translates to what? That you're going to try and spear her?'

'Such an elegant way of putting it.'

He'd been wrong about himself. He wasn't an ass sometimes. He was an ass *all* the time. He was perfect for heading up a parish committee. Such posts usually go to pious hypocrites like him.

'I'm not here to talk about your wife, Wilson. I'm here to

find out what the hell you were doing in Father Daly's motel room the other night.'

'That's a damned lie. I wasn't anywhere near there.'

'I've got an eyewitness who says you were. An eyewitness any district attorney would love to put on the stand.'

Right, I thought. And just pray Tommy Hubbard didn't bring up his association with the Rangers or mention the fact that he probably hadn't been gainfully employed for several years.

Wilson sipped his scotch and stared at me.

Then, quietly, he said: 'You're not bluffing, are you?'

'No, I'm not.'

'It was that sonofabitch two doors down, wasn't it? Some old deadbeat, right? I saw the bastard out of the corner of my eye. I just kept on walking.'

'Why were you there?'

'None of your business.'

'Legally, you're right. I don't have any authority to make you explain yourself to me. But I can always call the police.'

He waved a thick angry hand. 'For her. For Ellie. Why the hell else would I go out there?'

'Why for Ellie? Why did she need help?'

'She wasn't going to see him any more. She couldn't take the way he was obsessed with her. They never slept together or anything like that – she wouldn't let it go that far. But she was pissed at me for one of my little escapades and so she started seeing him as a counselor and then one thing led to another and he was in love with her.'

He shook his head. 'They're all fucking crazy at that rectory. Father Ryan yells at people in the confessional and Father Daly wasn't happy unless he was getting parish women to fall in love with him, and even your friend the Monsignor—' He stopped himself.

'What about my friend, the Monsignor?'

He shrugged. 'He's a piss poor leader. Only reason the Archbishop gave him the gig is because he used to be such a big deal in sports – Steve Gray, I mean. All the talk going around about priests being fags and child molesters, the Archbishop figured it'd be a good thing to have a sports hero for a Monsignor. Strictly PR. Your friend Gray couldn't run a fucking one-pump gas station, let alone a big parish like St Mallory's. *I* run the god-damned thing. And even he'd tell you that if he wanted to be truthful.'

'You didn't finish telling me why you were in Father Daly's room the other night.'

He sipped some more scotch then sat back, visibly relaxing as he did so. He must have felt in control again.

'He called her early in the evening, Daly did. I picked up and listened to them talk.'

'There's nothing like privacy.'

'Hey, the guy's trying to fuck my wife. Why should I give him any privacy?'

'You think Ellie listens in when your bimbos call?'

He sulked. Nobody had treated him this badly in a long time.

'Look, asshole, what I do is my business. You understand?'

'What did Father Daly say on the phone?'

He sighed. 'Said he needed to talk to her. Said he just wanted her to come out for a little while. To the Palms. The room he usually had. Anyway, she did. She felt sorry for him. He gave her a whole raft of shit about how he'd leave the priesthood and run away with her, if she'd agree to divorce me. The sonofabitch was so pathetic, he got her to give him one of her earrings. As a memento, he said. She got home and I confronted her and she told me everything and I decided to go out and pay him a visit myself. Which I did. I wanted to tell him to keep away from my wife, or I'd call the Archbishop of the Hilton diocese – this diocese – and Father Daly would be out.'

'And he said what to all this?'

Another sigh. 'He didn't say anything. He was dead when I got there.'

'Describe the scene.'

'What?'

'Tell me exactly what you saw when you got there.'

He told me. Nothing much had changed from what I'd observed when I'd met Steve Gray out there.

'Then what did you do?'

'I went and had a couple of drinks at a bar. I was real shook-up and confused. Then I just drove home.'

'Why didn't you call the police?'

'Are you crazy? I didn't want to get involved.'

'You have any idea who killed him?' I said.

'None.'

'Maybe Ellie killed him.'

'Don't be ridiculous.'

'It's always a possibility,' Ellie said, coming back into the room. Her glass was filled with the same amber liquid her husband was drinking.

She came over and sat on the arm of his chair. 'I could have killed him, Bob.'

'Could have. But didn't.'

She caressed his hand. 'Or maybe you killed him.'

'I was mad enough to but I didn't.'

She took his hand and set it on her very nice thigh, his big possessive bear paw of a hand, and when I saw them sitting there like that, I once again felt like a rube, because there was something that I profoundly didn't understand about their relationship. For all her complaints, she clearly got some kind of satisfaction from being with him; and for all his faithlessness, he was still caught up with her.

Or maybe there was some kind of spiritual S&M that I didn't *want* to know about in their relationship.

'I didn't kill him, Payne,' Wilson said. 'Just to put your mind at ease.'

'And I didn't kill him either, Robert,' Ellie said in her nice, quiet, polite voice.

'I don't think he believes us, dear,' Wilson, and then let out with one of his looming laughs.

I set down my glass and stood up.

'I'll be going.'

'He's pissed,' Wilson said.

'Bob, you've goaded him enough,' Ellie said. 'Then: 'Let me walk you to the door, Robert.'

'No, thanks,' I said.

I started walking.

'Or maybe I did kill him, Payne,' Wilson said from behind me. 'Maybe I was drunk and I just don't *remember* killing him.'

The booming laugh again.

'Oh Bob, for God's sake,' Ellie said. But there was fondness and tolerance in the voice, not derision.

I closed the front door behind me and walked out into full star-scattered night.

I could still hear him in the house, laughing.

Suddenly, the air up here didn't feel anywhere near as clean as it once had. This was a family with some secrets I probably didn't want to know about. Maybe being a rube sometimes isn't so bad after all. Maybe it's a form of protection.

And they'd succeeded in getting me too riled to remember to ask why Wilson didn't take the earring with him the first time he was there.

I'd need to do some more thinking about that. Right now I didn't *want* to ask.

iii

I didn't want to go home. I didn't want to get in an argument with Felice. I didn't want to see Vic again, or be shushed because he was sleeping.

I went to my office at the law firm, got out a yellow legal pad, and started doing what I was trained to do. On paper, this time, not on the computer.

I was going to create a psychological profile, that wasn't going to be worth jack shit because I couldn't get my hands on a tenth of the information I needed.

One murder. Father Daly.

Father Daly was a womanizer. Steve told me he'd had affairs with two women. Women he was counseling, which made it a violation of two different codes of ethics.

Other people had told me about more women. Ten or twelve. Or more ass than a toilet sees.

I'd never know how many women he'd been with. I doubted he knew himself.

Father Ryan heard him on the phone with a woman about 11:00 P.M. Daly was still home at midnight. He checked into the motel shortly after midnight.

Who'd been in his room? Ellie Wilson. Bob Wilson. And probably somebody else. Maybe several somebodies else.

Ellie's earring was there. Her husband didn't take it the

first time he was in the room. He took it *after* I'd seen it, and Steve had seen it. Why?

How did he know Steve would be called at all? For all he knew, the police might have been first on the scene. If they were, then he wouldn't stand the chance of a snowball in hell of ever getting the earring back.

Why didn't it matter if the police saw the earring, but it did matter if Steve and I did?

Well, that made sense. He didn't know me, but he knew Steve, and Steve might recognize the earring.

The other earring falls out of her purse. Wilson grabs it from me and puts it back in the purse. He knows I've seen both earrings and doesn't care, so long as I didn't actually have them in my custody.

Were there two earrings?

Or was this the only earring, and did she and her husband both want me to think it was two earrings, so she dropped her purse on purpose?

Why?

Because Bob Wilson *was* the murderer, and the earrings – or earring – were supposed to make me think Ellie had done it, and then after I'd told the police and Ellie had been arrested, Ellie was going to pop up with a perfect alibi?

Because Bob Wilson had left the earring there on purpose to suggest to the cops that a woman was the killer?

Then why would it be okay for the *cops* to see the earring . . .

I shook my head. I was thinking in circles.

Back up.

Tawanna Jackson was stabbed to death in Bowker Park. Her eyes were gouged out. She occasionally attended services at St Mallory's with her family; her mother had been a devout worshipper there.

Ronald Swanson was stabbed to death behind a bar. His ear was cut off. He was the father of three children. He went to church at St Mallory's . . .

Father Daly was stabbed to death in a motel room. His

170

tongue was cut out. He could have been the father of some natural children – it wasn't impossible, but nobody had mentioned it to me, and amidst all the other scandal I had been told about him, somebody would have mentioned it. But he was called Father.

He was a priest at St Mallory's.

He was a counselor. But neither Jackson nor Swanson had been in counseling.

No. But it was inevitable that at some time, they had visited the confessional . . .

What was Tawanna Jackson not supposed to see? Or, alternately, what had she seen that she shouldn't have seen?

What was Ronald Swanson not supposed to hear? Or, alternately, what had he heard that he shouldn't have heard?

What was Father Daly not supposed to tell? Or what had he told that he shouldn't have told?

The confessional.

He wasn't allowed to tell anybody what he had heard in the confessional.

But whoever killed Ronald Swanson, whoever killed Tawanna Jackson, might not trust him.

He had known something that he couldn't be allowed to tell.

And recently, somebody had bearded him in the cabin about it, and he and that somebody had quarrelled. He'd said – what was it Kevin Ward told me? – *This is insane. This is really insane. Don't you know that? Don't you realize what you're doing?*

He knew who had done the other killings. Had quarrelled with the killer at the cabin. But wasn't murdered there. Why?

Who would have known he was at the cabin?

Father Ryan. Steve. Jenny? Bernice?

Ellie Wilson? Bob Wilson?

And what about Michael Grady, who had drowned? Was he a piece of this puzzle or a piece of another puzzle altogether?

Did Father Daly just collect clippings about people he knew?

Or – and this is rare, but not unheard of – did I have two serial killers working together, using different methods of operation?

Or two serial killers working at the same time but *not* working together?

And Father Daly knew about both of them?

This was stretching too far even for a hypothesis. Except – *the confessional*. What might Father Daly have heard in the confessional? I kept going back to that.

All right, say it was two people working together.

Say it was Bob Wilson *and* Ellie Wilson . . . They were screwed up enough, that was for sure. But why, and how – and which one of them did the screwy murders and which one did the ordinary ones?

Ellie Wilson could *not* have cut out a man's tongue. Of that, I was sure. Bob Wilson could have, but was his mind screwy enough to dream that up? I didn't really think so. A simple bashing – yes, he was capable of that. But this murderer – or these murderers – were too subtle for that.

There are things you learn from what you see at the crime scene. There are things you learn from what you *don't* see at the crime scene – and this concept is hard for a lot of people – even cops – to understand.

This killer would be, in some ways, the Ted Bundy type: intelligent, suave, charming, probably living with his family or in some other settled lifestyle. Probably he'd been harshly disciplined in childhood, but the results of it wouldn't show on the surface. This profile looked more and more like it was fitting Ellie – except how would she have come across the other victims? By their serving with her husband on the parish council? Even so, why would she have killed them?

He – or she – or they – would get along well in the real world. The crimes would have been planned, not impulsive.

The crimes would be the result of a situation.

He might be chosen by God to wipe out all Catholics, or he might be trying to cover up some other crime, but the reasons

172

would make sense to him. And to anybody else who accepted his logic.

He'd be likely to return to the crime scene. He'd be likely to get along well with the investigators, to offer whatever information he had or wanted the investigators to think he had, maybe even to call the police himself (but each body had been discovered, and reported, by someone different).

And he – or she – had some very strong connection with St Mallory's, and specifically with the rectory. Which meant that was where I was going now.

Fast.

Before he invented a fourth wise monkey: *know* no evil.

And that wise monkey, come to think of it, might turn out to be me.

iv

I'd start with Jenny, I thought, because of all the possibles she fit the profile the least. She wasn't suave. She wasn't mentally well-organized. She'd be more likely to kill out of impulse than to plan. She hadn't been placed at any of the crime scenes even once, much less twice. So she could, perhaps, answer some more questions for me.

Of course, she was the only one who had tried to stab anybody. I'd better keep my wits about me.

I parked in back of the rectory and went up the walk on the side and knocked on the back door.

Through the glass, I could see Bernice talking to Father Ryan. He was drinking a can of 7-Up. She was shrugging into her coat.

At my knock, she walked over to the door, peered out, saw me, and opened up.

'Just in time for a late dessert,' she said. 'I made the Fathers an apple pie, which is my specialty. If I do say so myself.'

The kitchen was a friendly place, warm and well-lighted against the falling darkness. The linoleum was old and faded but the appliances were shiny new.

'She's being modest,' Father Ryan said. He wore a plaid shirt and jeans. 'Her apple pie is world-class.'

She winked at me. 'He has to say that if he wants me to make another one tomorrow.'

175

She glanced around the kitchen. 'Well, everything seems in shape here. I guess I can go now. Jenny is here if you need anything, Father.'

Those were her words. Her *meaning*, given the tone of her voice, was that Jenny was a poor substitute for the real thing, that being Bernice, of course.

'Night, Father.'

'Night, Bernice. Thanks for everything.'

'My pleasure, Father. Night, Mr Payne.'

'Night, Bernice.'

After she left, Father Ryan said, 'I was just about to call the Monsignor down for a piece of pie. Care to join us? There's plenty.'

'Thanks, anyway, Father. Actually, I came to talk to Jenny, if that's possible.'

'She's got the room in the basement. There's a bell you can ring to let her know you're coming down. I can show you where it is.'

'Great.'

He led me out of the well-lighted kitchen halfway down a hall to a door.

'The basement,' he said. Then he pointed to a small aluminum circle. 'And the bell.'

'Thanks again.'

'If you need anything, we'll be in the dining room, which is right down the hall.'

I rang the bell twice, opened the door, clipped on the light switch, and went down the stairs.

The basement was big but standard, furnace in one corner, washer and dryer in another, twenty or so cardboard boxes piled up next to the large wooden room built against the east wall. The floor was dry, the walls showing no signs of moisture or mildew. The basement even smelled clean.

Jenny came out of the room's door in a nubby pink terry-cloth robe. She wore no shoes. Her feet were small and cute, like fetching little animals. She was drying her wet hair with a white towel.

'This is a surprise,' she said. 'A nice one.'

'I just wanted to talk to you a little bit.'

She looked disappointed. 'Oh. I was hoping you'd come to see *me*. You know, just because you liked me. But it's about Father Daly, isn't it?'

'I'm afraid it is.'

'Well, maybe we could spend a few minutes talking about him, and then spend a few minutes talking about something else.'

Her one-room apartment was surprisingly cozy. There was a handsome couch that could be made into a bed at night-time, a 19" color TV on a stand, a small bookcase packed with Star Trek paperbacks, and one of those portable man-high closets made of pressed wood. The lone table-lamp next to the armchair cast flattering shadows over the room. The one problem was the cigarette smoke lying gray and harsh on the air.

'This is a nice place.'

'That's why I don't want Bernice to get me fired.'

'I don't think Bernice wants to get you fired.'

'I thought you were on my side.' Betrayal was strong in her voice.

'I'm not on anybody's side, Jenny. But I don't think Bernice is trying to get you fired.'

I saw a brief moment of junkie madness in her eyes, that druggy paranoia that never fails to impress or frighten me.

'She got to you, didn't she?'

'I guess I don't know what that means.'

'Sure you know what it means, Robert. Told you her side of the story. Made herself out to be this long-suffering saint and me to be this little slut who was always coming on to Father Daly.'

'Were you always coming on to Father Daly?'

'I was going to invite you to sit down, Robert. Now I don't think I will.'

'Will you answer my question, Jenny? *Were* you always coming on to Father Daly?'

She sighed. 'I wanted to sleep with him. That, I admit. And that was probably wrong. I mean, in a weird way, he really did take his vows seriously.' She sighed again and looked me straight in the eye. 'I suppose a few times I did come on to him. You want to sit down?'

'Thanks.'

I saw down.

'She was jealous – Bernice, I mean.'

'I see.'

She watched me a moment. 'Boy, she really did get to you, didn't she?'

She sat down on the couch. Slowly. Carefully. As if she might fall. She looked pale and tired suddenly. 'I thought you and I were going to be friends. You know, really mean something to each other. But now I see—'

She stopped. Tears shone in her eyes.

'But now you see what, Jenny?' I said gently.

'Now I see that you're just like everybody else I've ever known.' She put her head back, tears streaming down her cheeks, and placed both of her hands over her heart. It should have been a melodramatic gesture but here, now, there was something pure and child-like and touching about it.

'All my life I've had so much fucking love to give some-body, and nobody would ever take it. Not my mother or father or my sister or my friends at school. I used to think that people knew something about me that I didn't know. You know, they realized that there was something really wrong with me that I couldn't see. I always felt alone. Always. And I'd cry a lot for no reason at all. Just fucking weep. And then when I was fifteen, I discovered junk. And everything was cool then, everything was all right.'

She stopped talking, brought her head back down level, and then wiped tears away with a single delicate finger.

'But now I don't have junk to lean on any more, and it's really scary.' Then: 'You know the funny thing?'

'What?'

'He was a lot like me. Father Daly. The way he loved Ellie

Wilson. I think he wanted to give her everything he felt, too. But she wouldn't let him. Personally, I always thought she was just sort of leading him on, that she thought it was kind of flattering to have a priest fall in love with you. Especially a handsome young one like Father Daly. I mean, Monsignor Gray and Father Ryan both warned him about what he was doing but he didn't seem to care. One night he went crazy and started yelling at Father Ryan about something and then another night he shoved Monsignor Gray real hard against the wall.'

'Was he drinking?'

'No. But he had a temper. The Monsignor said something to him, something I didn't catch, and that was when Father Daly got so mad.'

Then: 'Sometimes I think I was happier back in the halfway house.'

'That was one of the things I wanted to talk to you about.'

'Oh?'

'The halfway house.'

She said, 'You found out, huh?'

'Found out?'

'About that night with the knife.'

'Yeah, I guess I did.'

'I'm not sure I really would've stabbed him. I mean, I really loved him. But he's just like you are – all wrapped up in your own problems, and not the least bit interested in me.'

'He dropped the charges.'

'That's only because he was afraid of what I was going to tell the police.'

'And what was that?'

She sighed. Looked away for a moment.

'That we were having sex.'

'I see.'

'I mean, not actual screwing. But blow jobs. He was always having me give him blow jobs.'

'So he was afraid—'

'He has a wife and two kids. He knew it'd come out in the

papers, what we were doing I mean, if he actually went ahead and pressed charges, so—'

'So he didn't press charges.'

'Right,' she said. Then she smiled tearfully: 'I've led a pretty exemplary life, don't you think?'

I smiled. 'None of us has led an exemplary life, Jenny.'

While she'd been talking so animatedly, her terrycloth robe had gaped, partially exposing her nicely shaped breasts.

She saw where my eyes had strayed and smiled.

'We could make love and they wouldn't hear us.'

'I don't think that's such a good idea, Jenny.'

'Would you come over here and put your arm around me?'

'I guess I could do that.'

So I went over and sat down next to her and put my arm around her. Her hair smelled wet and clean, exhilarating, and her flesh thrummed with youth and sex.

'You think I killed him?' she said.

'It's a possibility.'

'Sometimes I think I did. I *wanted* to. I mean, I really thought about it a lot.'

'Did you know he was at the motel room?'

'Sure.'

'Sure?'

'Yeah. I used to follow him out there. Whenever he was gone from the rectory very long, I always assumed that's where he went.'

It happened so quickly, there was nothing I could do, her arms around me, her tongue in my mouth.

I didn't want to stop it. She was a desirable young woman and my need was suddenly enormous. I felt her soft breasts against my chest. The touch of her wet hair was erotic and overpowering. Then she was guiding my hand down inside her robe—

I pushed away.

Thinking I'd heard something just outside the door.

'No, please,' she said, struggling to keep me in her embrace. There was a frenzy about her now.

I suppose it took me a full minute to get up on my feet and move to the door.

I looked across the basement, then to the steps that angled up the far wall. While I saw nothing, I heard the basement door closing quietly.

I went back to the couch. Her entire body was shaking. I wondered if she was having some kind of seizure. I held her as tightly as I could.

I don't know how long we sat there, it could have been three or four hours the slow sad way the moments ticked by, and then she put her face into my shoulder and began sobbing.

I held her even tighter now.

I thought of some Dylan Thomas lines from one of my college lit. courses: 'When lovers lie abed/Their arms wrapped round the grief of the ages.' She was one of those women whose embrace would always be wrapped round such grief.

Then a voice was calling my name – Steve Gray's. There was a phone call for me. Upstairs. In his study.

Brad Doucette was on the phone.

'Ellie Wilson's been calling here the last half hour. Three times. She really wants to talk to you.'

'About what? I was just out there.'

'About what? You haven't heard?'

Then he told me.

I hung up. 'Do you have Ellie Wilson's number?' I asked Steve.

'What's wrong, Robert?' he said, thumbing through the Rolodex on his desk.

I said, 'Detective Holloway just brought Bob Wilson in for questioning. I think Holloway thinks Wilson is the killer.'

V

The lawyer's name was Harry Solomon. He was generally considered to be Brad Doucette's only serious competition in local criminal law.

He was in the waiting area at the front of the police station trying to calm Ellie Wilson. When I called the number Steve Gray gave me, I'd been transferred to the phone in Ellie's car. She said she'd meet me at the police station.

Harry Solomon was a tall, slightly stooped man with a handsome, even distinguished face, and a shaggy white band of hair around his otherwise bald head. He wore a red windbreaker, chinos and penny-loafers. He recognized me from the times he'd seen me with Brad. He offered a quick, strong hand.

'I was just telling Ellie that Bob would have to spend the night here,' Solomon said. 'I've already talked to the judge. He's set bail and now it's just a matter of paperwork.'

'Where's Bob?' I said.

'Upstairs. In an interrogation room,' Solomon said. 'I'm due up there in a few minutes. Right now I'm more worried about Ellie than I am about Bob.'

She looked completely forlorn, sitting very primly on a bench that faced a pebbled glass door reading DETECTIVE DIVISION.

'This is all my fault,' she said with no inflection whatsoever,

183

as if she'd memorized it and were speaking by rote. 'I never should have gone to see Father Daly that night.'

'Ellie, listen,' Solomon said, leaning down and taking her frail hands in his big purposeful ones. 'You've told me that Bob isn't guilty, and Bob's told me that, too. And that being the case, we're going to be all right.'

She looked up at him with frightened eyes. 'But innocent people are found guilty all the time.'

'Not as often as you probably think, Ellie,' Solomon said. 'What you need to do is relax. I know that's not easy in these circumstances, but you have to try. You don't want Bob to see you like this. That's not going to help him any, is it?'

She smiled up at him, patted his hand gratefully. He was for this moment her very favorite uncle.

'You're right, Harry. I need to be in control of myself, don't I?'

I heard footsteps coming around the far corner. Detective Holloway appeared, walking quickly, spritzing her inhalant into her right nostril.

I walked over to her so we could talk privately.

She wore a red turtleneck and a pair of stonewashed jeans. She carried her piece on a small holster attached to the left side of her belt.

'It gets worse at night,' she said, taking the white plastic inhaler from her nostril. 'You should hear my poor kids when they're sleeping.' Her nose and eyes were red from pollen.

'You brought Bob Wilson in for questioning?'

'I sure did.'

And with that, she sneezed again, and went over to grab Harry Solomon.

When I sat down next to Ellie, she said, 'He didn't do it.'

When I didn't say anything, she said, 'Don't you believe me?'

'Right now I don't believe anything in particular. There's a lot in the air.'

'A lot of what?'

'Odds and ends. Things that might mean something but then again might not.'

'Like what?'

'Oh, like the fact that Jenny at the rectory almost stabbed her counselor two years ago. A prosecuting attorney might say that shows a predisposition to violent behavior. And then there's a bunch of newspaper clippings that belonged to Father Daly. I haven't figured out what they mean yet. Maybe they mean nothing. And then there's you and your husband. And the man who heard Father Daly arguing with somebody out at the fishing cabin.'

'You really think one of us could have done that?'

'It's a possibility.'

'That's a terrible thing to say.'

'You were in his room. So was your husband.'

'Oh, God,' she said, remorse gripping her like a seizure. 'I started this whole mess, didn't I?'

'The mess between Bob and Father Daly? Yes, you probably did.'

She put her hands together and sat very still. She looked as if she wanted a magic bus to come and pick her up and take her far, far away.

'The Monsignor hated him,' she said softly.

'Hated Father Daly?'

'Yes.'

'Why?'

'Father Daly knew something about him.'

'I don't know what that means.'

'Neither do I. He never told me what it was exactly. But every once in a while, after they'd had an argument, Father Daly would say, "One call to the Archbishop, and Monsignor Gray'll be out in the boonies" '.

'Why didn't they like each other?'

'There's a schism in the Church. The old-style Catholics versus the new-style Catholics. Father Daly was new-style. He used to make fun of Monsignor Gray to his face, especially when they were conducting religious classes together.

185

He wasn't just showing off – Father Daly, I mean. He really believed that the Monsignor's style of religion was very destructive. Heaven and hell and all that. Father Daly thought that religion should be more like science. Believe in the here and now and how we treat each other. Not worry about the old myths so much.'

'I could see where that would rankle Steve.'

'He's a nice man, Robert, but not the brightest person I've ever met.'

'Fat John.'

'Pardon?'

'That's what they used to say about the Pope they called Fat John. A very decent man but not a genius. He got a lot done, though, for not being a genius.'

'It was more style than anything – the Monsignor and Father Daly, I mean.'

'Style – and something that Father Daly might have been holding over Steve's head.'

'You should ask him.'

'I plan to.'

She touched my sleeve. 'I'm fighting for my husband's sake. I – he could have done it. His temper—'

'I know.'

'But *could have* is very different from *did*.'

'I know that, too.' I stood up. 'You could be here for a long time.'

She nodded. 'My time to pay a little dues, I guess.'

She looked like a sad angel.

'I'll probably talk to you tomorrow,' I said.

'I want you to keep working on the case – harder than ever now. That's why I called you. I've already put a check in the mail for two thousand dollars.'

She tried to smile but it didn't quite work. Not tonight. She just looked weary.

I put a hand on her shoulder and nodded good night.

186

vi

When I was finished working on the computer, I called Gilhooley.

Even before I heard him say hello, the receiver was filled with the ear-pounding noise of Cream playing *White Room*.

The only records Gilhooley owned dated from the late sixties and seventies. By now the surfaces of those records sounded as if they'd been worked over with steel wool. The hissing was louder than the music, but this didn't seem to bother Gilhooley any. Night after night, the ghosts of Janice and Jimi and Jim Morrison appeared in his book-littered living room.

'You think you could turn that down a little?' I said. Gilhooley can irritate me as few other people can. I have the same effect on him.

'I can hear *you* just fine,' he said.

'Well, I can't hear you.'

'Just a minute,' he said

I heard him pad away. I heard the music turned down. I heard him pad back to the phone.

'That's better. Thank you.'

'You're getting to be an old lady, Robert.'

'Well, hopefully an old lady with her hearing still intact.'

'I wish Cream would reunite,' he said.

'I wish the Monkees would reunite.'

'I know that's supposed to be a joke, Robert, but all that bullshit commercial music you listen to, I wouldn't be surprised if you *did* wish the Monkees would reunite.'

To him, Steely Dan is bullshit commercial music.

I said, 'I just wonder how your background checks are going.'

'Well, I'm mostly picking up odds and ends.'

'I'm listening.'

'This Father Ryan?'

'Uh-huh.'

'Very bad temper. Yells at people in the confessional.'

'That one I'm aware of.'

'You *were* kidding about the Monkees, weren't you?'

'I'm not even going to answer that stupid question.'

'Wow. You had me worried.' Then: 'And your friend, Monsignor Gray?'

'What about him?'

'Last year at this time, he sold his brand-new Chrysler – that he'd just bought a few months earlier – to raise cash.'

I thought of what Ellie Wilson had told me about Father Daly 'having something' on Steve.

'Any idea why he needed to raise cash?' I said.

'Not that I've been able to find so far.'

'Anything else?'

'The housekeeper Bernice?'

'Uh-huh.'

'Both she and this Father Ryan wrote letters to the Archbishop about Father Daly.'

'How the hell'd you find *that* out?'

'Got an uncle who works for the Archbishop.'

'You know what the letters said?'

'No, but I assume they didn't have the desired effect.'

'What desired effect?'

'Well, presumably, the only reason they'd write to the Archbishop was to get rid of Daly, right?'

'Right.'

'And this was nearly a year ago now.'

'Right.'

'So,' he said, 'if they were trying to get rid of Father Daly, they obviously didn't succeed.'

I wondered why neither Bernice or Father Gray had told me about the letters they'd sent to the Archbishop.

'One more thing.'

'All right,' I said.

'This Ellie Wilson? Last four months she's been quietly liquidating a lot of her stock and other holdings.'

'You're kidding.'

'Nope. Got a good friend at one of the stock brokerages downtown.'

'Does her husband know about this?'

'No idea. But the way my friend explained it, the Wilson woman's keeping all of this very quiet.'

A quick scenario crossed my mind. Wife tired of bullying husband. Liquidates considerable holdings. Kills somebody and frames husband for it. After husband sentenced to prison, wife has plenty of money for travel and lavish life-style. Wife has freedom *and* money.

But then what did the previous murders have to do with this?

I didn't like flying blind.

'You're doing great work, Gilhooley. I appreciate it.'

'You know, the more I think about it, the more you probably *did* like the Monkees.'

'Very funny,' I said. 'Ha ha.'

When I got home, Felice was asleep. I knew better than to wake her.

5:

POLICE DEPARTMENT

Frank Earle Mason
Age: 43
Race: Caucasian
Occupation: Paint-store owner
Marital Status: M
Military Service: Army, 1973-75,
Honorable dis.

Mason: This is about money and nothing else.
           She's got herself a lawyer, doesn't she?
           People see you have a little cash stashed
           away and they want part of it. And as
           for me 'coercing her' . . . that's total
           bullshit. This little gal has been around,
           believe me. This virginal bit is bullshit.
           For one thing, you'll notice that she
           doesn't say we ever actually screwed
           because we didn't. Now, I'll admit that
           maybe in fun a couple of times I said,
           'Marie, you got a couple kids and no
           husband at home, it sure would be
           terrible you lose your job down here.' So
           she gave me a few blow jobs, what's all
           this sexual harassment horseshit
           anyway?

Frank Mason

Tuesday the blue Ford is there again, parked up on the hill behind the trailer park.

Sixteen-year-old Frank Mason stands at the bedroom window of his own trailer. Frank's a big kid, lots of shaggy yellow hair and a snotty grin for everybody he feels superior to – which means just about everybody he crosses path with – and now Frank's got his binoculars to his eyes and he's watching the guy hurrying down the path from the hill to the last row of trailers back near the creek.

Guy obviously thinks he's being real cool and sneaky.

Like nobody's aware of what he's doing.

Well, big Frank is aware of what he's doing, and in fact Frank's got plans that aren't going to make the guy happy at all.

'What the hell you doin', Frank?' his old man says from the hallway, echoes of the toilet flushing still filling Frank's ears.

No living thing can approach the toilet now for a good twenty minutes. The stench is just something terrible, Camels and turds, the old man's specialty.

'I'm lookin' through your binoculars.'

'You give me those right now.'

He puts his hand out, palm up. Like Frank is really going to hand over the binoculars.

Yeah, right.

'You know the trouble you got into watchin' Dottie with

those damned things,' the old man says.

Dottie being this babe who lives two trailers away. At night, Frank used to spy on her, look right in her window when she was undressing, till one night one of the kids playing night-tag around the trailers saw Frank . . . and told Dottie. She came over all red-faced and pissed, screaming she was a decent woman, and screaming she was going to call the cops, and screaming that Frank was nothing but a bully, the way he treated everybody in the trailer park but he wasn't gonna treat her that way, no sir he wasn't.

It was worth all the hassle, Dottie's tits being what they are, but the old man and the old lady really got on him about it, and in fact the old man hid the binoculars from him once and for all.

But last week, Frank found where the old man had put them – up in the closet with all the porno playing cards he got back in his Navy days – and he's had the binoculars ever since.

'You give me those.'

Frank grins. 'How about you take 'em from me?'

'You think I can't, you mouthy little prick?'

Frank throws the binoculars on the bed and then puts up his dukes, in a parody of the way they did back when boxers went at each other bare-knuckled.

He starts boxing around the old man, feinting left, feinting right, grinning, laughing, enjoying watching the old man come all undone, finally shooting a roundhouse right that makes the old man jerk scared out of the way.

'C'mon. Just two rounds.' Frank is laughing his ass off. 'Just two rounds. C'mon, Dad, put 'em up.'

The old man is wheezing all of a sudden. Emphysema. That was the diagnosis six months ago. And it's getting worse all the time.

The old man falls against the frame of the doorway, panting now.

'Aw, shit,' Frank says. 'You aren't any fun any more.'

He takes the old man's right arm and gets under it and helps carry the old man into the living room and lay him down on the couch. The old man is coughing now, too. The coughing drives Frank nuts. All day, all night. Coughing.

The old lady spends as much time at her sister's as she can. Can't take the old man's coughing.

'You stay there now, hear me?'

'You don't be lookin' at Dottie any more.'

'You leave Dottie to me,' Frank grins, trying to give the old man the impression that he just may take another gander at Dottie's naked tits after all.

The old man lapses into cursing again.

Frank goes back to his window. And his binoculars.

Later that same day, Frank takes a shower and splashes on some Old Spice and tip-toes past the old man. He's snoring.

Frank goes outside and stands smoking a Lucky. Nice, warm summer day. Ninety-two degrees. Takes another deep drag, enjoying himself. The little kids playing in the sandy road between the rows of trailers watch him warily. To them, Frank is the scariest guy in the trailer park.

Frank stamps out his cigarette then turns around and starts walking between the trailers, back to where the creek runs.

The guy in the blue Ford left an hour ago.

Frank reaches the door of the trailer and knocks. Jinny, that's the seven-year-old daughter, stands in the screen door, saying nothing, just watching Frank. A country-music singer cries out on the radio.

'Whyn't you come out and play, Jinny?' Frank says. 'There's a lot of kids in the road out there.'

'My mom don't want me to. Says I should stay inside when it's this hot.' She's tugging on her pigtails idly.

Then he hears her mother coming. 'Who is it, Jinny?'

'Frank says I should go outside and play, Mom.'

Then she's there. Technically, she's a little too old, Sandy Thompson, thirty-six her last birthday. Too old for somebody Frank's age anyway, but she has a wonderfully fleshy body, one he's seen several times in a two-piece bikini when she lies out by the creek sunning herself. While her hubby Sam puts in his eight hours down at the paint factory.

197

Frank says, 'Whyn't you let her go play?'

'It's too hot. And it's not your business anyway.'

Frank smiles. 'Is it the business of the guy in the blue Ford?'

She freezes. Just for a moment. She is wearing a pink polo shirt with a bra and a pair of Levi cut-offs. In addition to her sumptuous tits, she's got silken legs.

Frank stares at her steadily. 'You sure you won't change your mind and let her go play? Seems like you and me ought to have a little talk.'

Jinny looks up at her mom. 'Can I, Mom? Frank says there's a lot of kids in the road.'

Sandy sighs. 'All right. But not for very long.'

'Goody!' Jinny says, clapping her hands together. She bolts from the door.

The door slams after her. Sandy just stands on the other side of it, staring at him.

'You gonna tell Sam?'

'Who is he? The guy in the Ford?'

'My first husband. Jinny's father.'

Frank grins. 'Now isn't that cozy.'

'He dumped me and I never got over him. Loved him ever since second grade, if you can picture that.' She shakes her head. 'Now he got dumped by the woman he left me for. He's real heartbroken. So I do what I can for him.'

'I bet you do.'

'But I feel shitty about it. Sam's a good man. He works hard. Don't miss a day of work even when he's sick as a dog. He knows I don't love him and he don't even care. He just says that someday I'll love him. And now I'm doin' this to him, sneakin' around like some whore, I mean.'

'You going to invite me in?'

'You said your piece. You're going to tell Sam and there ain't much I can do about it.' Tears glisten in her eyes.

'Oh, there's something you can do about it, all right.'

Just now she's figured out why Frank is here. He never did plan to tell Sam.

★ ★ ★

They're in her bedroom, lying on her bed. He can't take his eyes off her breasts beneath the polo shirt.

'You do for me, I do for you, that's the way these things work.'

'You're just a kid.'

Smirks. 'Well, I guess I'll just have to show you how much of a kid I am.'

She's been crying again and her nose is red. 'But this'll just make it worse. Now I'll be cheatin' on Sam with *two* guys.'

'I guess you won't mind it then if I give Sam a call tonight . . .'

Then he reaches out and touches her breast. Her first response is to close her eyes, as if she's enduring great humiliation.

The eyes stay closed. 'It'll only be this one time, that we do it, I mean?'

'Just this one time,' Frank says.

'I only do it with my first husband cause I still love him.'

'What time you say Sam gets off?'

She opens her eyes again. 'I'm on the pill so that part's all right.'

And then he knows he's got her.

'Just this one time, you promise?'

'I promise.'

'And you won't tell Sam?'

'I won't tell Sam.'

'Cause it'd just kill him. And he don't deserve that.'

All the time he's on top of her, she's crying. But that doesn't bother Frank.

He plans on making this a long-term kinda thing. He'll see to it that she not only quits crying, she'll move that body of hers a lot more, too. Beautiful body like that and she just lays there like a corpse. Well, next time they get together, things are gonna be different.

Very, very different.

Five

i

Father Ryan said eight o'clock Mass. I knew this because I was there. I hadn't been to Confession in years so there was no Communion for me.

I just knelt in a rear pew smelling the incense and looking at the Stations of the Cross and watching the sweet old women make their arthritic way to and from the Communion rail. God had been so vivid to me when I was a boy. I knew what He expected of me and I knew what I expected of myself. I still believe in some kind of god, some guiding cosmic force, but I couldn't tell you anything about he/she/it. I especially couldn't tell you why it is so imperative that the forlorn lost tribes of this planet must endure so much heartbreak.

After Mass, I waited on the walk between the church and the rectory. The coos of pigeons echoed between the buildings. The air smelled good and clean and new. The sun was shining and I felt ridiculously young and strong, as only spring days can make me feel.

Father Ryan came out of the side door of the church in his cassock.

'Morning, Mr Payne.'

'Morning, Father.'

'If you're looking for the Monsignor, he's downtown. One of his committee meetings.'

'Actually, it was you I wanted to see.'

He smiled. 'Now that doesn't sound very good.'

'Just take a few minutes, is all.'

He checked his wrist-watch. 'If you're serious about it being just a few minutes, why don't we swing over to the school cafeteria? I've got a religion class to teach in fifteen minutes, but that's time enough for a quick cup of coffee. How's that sound?'

'Sounds great.'

As we headed back toward the alley, and the two-story red-brick school on the other side, he said, 'That's all they talk about.'

He nodded to a group of grade-school girls who were jumping rope. They wore plaid school uniforms with white blouses and blue knee-high socks.

'Why somebody would murder a priest, I mean,' he said. 'I taught six classes yesterday and that's all they talked about. And I didn't know what to tell them.'

The cafeteria had pretty much emptied out by the time we sat down with our coffee. This was a big, echoing gym that could be converted into a cafeteria quickly. Sunlight angled through the long, rectangular windows behind the bleachers.

The smell of cafeteria food took me on another time-machine ride. I saw myself as a small kid with a big tray and an even bigger appetite waiting calmly in line while all around me other kids shoved, goosed and slapped each other. I hadn't been the perfect kid, far from it. I just had this huge appetite. Luckily, I burned off the calories quickly.

'You know, this school almost closed down about ten years ago,' Father Ryan said, looking around at the dozen or so empty tables and the bright buff blue walls. 'Then private education came back into fashion, and now we're actually turning some students away. We're booked solid. And a lot of that's due to your friend, Monsignor Gray.'

'You seem to have a lot of respect for him.'

He nodded. 'I do. I mean, priests are just human beings

with a special calling. They have all the same foibles and shortcomings as any other human beings. I was at a parish for several years where all the man did was try to push his career ahead. The Monsignor isn't like that. He has a genuine concern for people – of all ages and all occupations. You run into a lot of priests who are snobs. They only want to know people like the Wilsons. You know, wealthy and involved in the parish. But the Monsignor ministers to everybody. He's a very impressive man.'

I looked at him carefully, keeping my voice as steady as possible. 'He have any secrets?'

He smiled. 'We all have secrets. I have a few that would curl your toes.'

'Serious secrets, I mean.'

'The Monsignor? Not that I know of.'

A gray-haired woman in a pink waitress uniform came over and refilled our cups.

After she'd gone, Father Ryan said, 'I feel sorry for Monsignor Gray.'

'Oh? Why?'

'He really deserves a much bigger parish than this one. More important, I mean. But this is a very political diocese and the Monsignor has never hidden his dislike of the Archbishop.'

'What's he got against the Archbishop?'

'Too media-savvy,' Father Ryan said. 'The Archbishop is a bit of a showboat, I'm afraid. Plus, nobody would ever accuse him of being a particularly intelligent man.'

'Steve ever have any run-ins with him?'

He smiled. 'You don't have "run-ins." You have memos. The Archbishop is always sending memos.'

'He sent Steve one?'

'One? One a month is more like it. The last one had to do with a newspaper article about the Monsignor. The reporter asked Steve about forgiving penitents – was there a sin so bad he *couldn't* forgive it? And Steve said, "As a priest, I have to grant absolution to all those who make a good Confession.

But that doesn't mean I can forgive them as a man." '

I set down my coffee cup. 'I'm having a little trouble of my own in the forgiveness department.'

'Oh?'

'My stepfather.'

'Those can be very bad relationships, very destructive, stepparents and stepchildren.'

I told him the situation.

'And he wants to stay with you?' he said.

'He says he wants to make up for all the years we lived together, when he never took much interest in me. But what's really going on is he's lonely and scared. The way he blusters and brags all the time, he doesn't have any friends left from the old days. I think he was the kind of guy who probably hit on the wives of his friends.'

'Even when he was married to your mother?'

'Sure.'

'He's a sinner and he's asking for forgiveness.'

'Yeah, I suppose he is.'

'How do you feel about that?'

I shrugged. 'I don't like him very much.'

'Well, then, I'd very gently suggest that you and he try to find a decent nursing home for him.'

'That isn't what Steve would do, is it?'

'Probably not,' he said. 'Steve would probably let him stay.'

'But you're not Steve.'

'No, I guess I'm not. I function on the belief that God gives us only what we can handle. It may not seem like it all the time, but it's true. And it doesn't sound like you can handle Vic being there. You've got a lot of resentment toward him.'

'That simple?'

'That simple.'

'But Steve wouldn't do it that way?'

'The Monsignor,' he said, 'is a special man. Very Christ-like, as I said. And I don't mean pious or sanctimonious. He's an old farmboy and always will be. Sanctimony embarrasses him, as a matter of fact.'

A bell rang in the hall outside the gym.

'That's for me,' Father Ryan said. 'My religion class.'

He walked me to the back door where we'd come in. 'I don't think Bob Wilson killed Father Daly.'

'I don't, either.'

'But I certainly don't think the Monsignor killed him, either,' he said. 'In case that's what you're thinking.'

'Right now, I don't know what I'm thinking, Father. I really don't.'

Even with the profile I'd created, that was true. There were people the profile fitted; there were people it didn't fit. But it wasn't complete, because my information wasn't complete.

Like flying in fog. A small plane, you fly by sight, just like you drive a car, and you can't fly it in fog. A bigger plane, you might fly blind, fly by instruments. But if you were in the fog, even if you did have instruments, if you didn't have the right coordinates you might come down dead.

I had the instruments. I'd honed them over thirteen years. But I didn't have all the coordinates.

We said goodbye, and I walked back to my car.

ii

Just as I was starting to slide into my car, I heard somebody call my name. I looked over and saw Bernice walking towards me, waving.

This morning she wore a pink blouse, royal-blue cardigan sweater, and royal-blue slacks. She also wore large sunglasses which gave her a slightly sexual edge she didn't usually have.

'Do you think he did it?' she said breathlessly.

'Bob Wilson, you mean?'

She nodded.

'I don't think so.'

'Then why did the police bring him in for questioning?'

'They probably know some things we don't. They certainly wouldn't bring him in on a whim.'

'He's an important man.'

'Exactly.' Then I said, 'Say, I was going to ask you to do me a favor.'

'Be glad to.' She smiled. 'Nice-looking young man like you.'

'I left all my quarters at home. Afraid I don't have anything to tip you with.'

'Here I go flattering you, and all you can talk about is tipping me.'

I leaned into my car and picked up a manila envelope into which I'd slipped copies of all the newspaper clippings.

'I wondered if you'd check these for me,' I said.

'Check them how?'

'Can you get into Father Daly's office?'

'I suppose so.'

'I've been trying to figure out why he kept these clippings. You know about them?'

She nodded. 'I heard he kept some clippings about people getting killed. Father Ryan and the Monsignor were talking about them. But I haven't seen them. Is that what these are?'

'Yes. And I started wondering if he knew the victims more than casually. I'd like to see if he knew them through his counseling.'

Father Ryan had told me he didn't. But Father Ryan fit the profile. So he might not have been telling the truth.

She took the envelope. 'I may not be able to get to it until later today, maybe not until this evening. Today is errand day at the rectory, you see. I'm usually gone most of the day.'

'Fine. My number's on the envelope there. Just call me when you find out. I'd really appreciate it. Oh, and don't mention it to Father Ryan. I don't want to worry him any more.'

She nodded.

We stood in the sunshine. Between church and rectory, the pigeons were still cooing. The school kids were back inside, having taken their laughter with them.

'It's interesting to watch a detective's mind at work,' she said. 'So if he was seeing these people professionally, and later on they were murdered, what do you think it could mean?'

'It *could* mean just about anything – or nothing.'

'It is sort of funny, though, isn't it, the way he kept these clippings?'

'Yeah, it is.'

'But there was always that part of him.'

'What part of him?'

'You know how, with some people, you can kind of get to know them real easy?'

I nodded.

'You never had that feeling with Father Daly. In fact, I always had the opposite feeling. I was never sure how he was going to react to things. He was very mysterious sometimes, and a little scary.'

'Did you ever see him lose his temper?'

She waggled a finger at me. 'You're thinking what I'm thinking, aren't you?'

'And what would that be, Bernice?'

'That maybe Father Daly killed these people. In the clippings, I mean.'

'I didn't say that.'

'No, but you were thinking it.'

'Why would he kill them?' I said.

'Oh, no. You're the detective. You tell me.'

'Well, I could take some guesses.'

But she was too excited to be quiet. 'First of all, were they all women?'

'No.'

'Did the men have wives? I mean, were they all married, the dead men?'

'Yes.'

'So there were women involved in all of the murders. And maybe they were all *attractive* women.'

'Maybe.'

'Well, let's say they were.'

'All right,' I said. 'They were all attractive women.'

'What if he forced himself on them?'

'What if he did? Why wouldn't they just go to the police?'

'Maybe they'd told him secrets – you know, things you'd tell an analyst. Maybe they were afraid he'd tell everybody what they'd told him. Am I getting anywhere?'

I laughed. 'You're pretty good at this.'

'You're just saying that.'

'No, you've got a very active imagination, and you're able to articulate your theories. That's what happens in group sessions at the FBI.'

'Really?'

'Really.'

'I can't wait to tell my grandchildren,' she said.

'There's just one problem, Bernice.'

'Problem?'

'If Father Daly did do what you said, who killed *him*?'

'You know, that's a very good point.'

'If you figure it out, let me know.'

'I guess that's where my theory falls down, huh, Robert?'

'Just keep working on it.'

She checked her watch. 'I've really got to run. This has been a lot of fun.' She waved the manila envelope at me, and then her smile died. 'If it just wasn't real. I'll be back to you sometime today.'

'Thanks. By the way, did you know Michael Grady?'

'The one that got drowned?'

'Right.'

'His funeral was here.' She looked disapproving. 'But he never could find time for the Church while he was alive.'

Twenty minutes later, I was pulling into a parking stall at the law firm.

'You've got somebody waiting for you in your office,' the receptionist said.

'Oh?'

She leaned forward so she could whisper. 'Beverly Wright.'

'Oh, great.'

Today Beverly wore a blue jumper with a white linen blouse. She looked young and fresh and maternal, the sort of pretty woman you see pushing a stroller in the park on sunny days.

'How are you today, Beverly?' I said, walking into the office.

'I'm not a whore.'

'I know you're not.'

'But that's what the county attorney's going to say about me, isn't it?'

Should I lie? Try to make things seem better than they were? 'Yeah, that's probably what he's going to say.'

'He wants to run for Governor in the primary. The county attorney, I mean.'

'That's what I hear.'

'So getting a guilty verdict would really make him look good, wouldn't it?'

'Aaron's a wealthy and important man.'

'That's another thing.'

'What is?'

'Don't juries like to convict wealthy, important men?'

'A lot of the time they do.'

'They'll really want to nail Aaron, won't they? I can see Aaron in court. He's got a bad temper and lot of people think he's pretty arrogant.'

'Aaron – arrogant?'

She matched my smile. 'But he can also be a very decent, tender man. He really can. He didn't work very hard at his marriage the last few years but his wife didn't, either. There's plenty of blame to go around.'

I nodded as I looked through my phone messages. Felice had called three times. I wondered if something was wrong. 'Beverly?'

'Yes?'

'I think we had this same conversation a few days ago, didn't we? You not being able to make up your mind?'

She chose to disregard my words.

'One thing his wife hated was that he'd never give her his undivided attention,' Beverly said. 'You know, like he'd read his phone messages while she was talking to him?'

'Guilty as charged,' I said, and sat up straight in my chair. 'You were saying?'

'I'm not a whore is what I was saying. But by the time the county attorney gets finished with me, that's how I'll come off.'

'Then you're not going to testify?'

'I talked to my son.'

'And what'd he say?'

'He gave me the same speech about right and wrong that I always give him.'

'So you *are* going to do it?'

She lifted narrow shoulders in a weary shrug. 'One minute I'm going to testify, the next minute I'm *not* going to testify.'

'I get like that.'

'Indecisive?'

'Sure.'

'An ex-FBI man?'

'Why shouldn't an ex-FBI man be just as indecisive as everybody else on the planet?'

'Well, I guess you've got a point there.'

'In fact, I knew a *lot* of really indecisive people when I was in the Bureau.'

'That really surprises me.'

'So what I'm saying,' I said, 'is that *you* shouldn't feel bad about being indecisive.'

'You're really a nice guy, you know that?'

'It's not easy, what we're asking you to do.'

'You'd like me to do it, wouldn't you?'

'Sure I would,' I said. 'But I'm not the one who has to sit in that witness chair in front of that whole courtroom of people.'

'I just thought of something.'

'What?'

'Is this reverse psychology?'

'I don't think so,' I said.

She shrugged again. 'God, I hate how cynical I am. You're a nice guy. Why can't I just accept that?'

'You want some coffee?'

'No, thanks. I've gotta go to pick up my son at baseball practice.' Then: 'Without me, they're probably going to nail him, aren't they?'

'Even with you, they might nail him.'

'You mean, even if I'd do it, it *still* might not help Aaron?'

'Uh-huh. Maybe the county attorney'll be able to convince the jury that you're lying to protect Aaron.'

212

'But I'm *not* lying.'

'I know you're not lying. But will the jury know that?'

'God, this is worse than it's ever been. Even if I help him, I may not help him is what you're saying?'

'It's a possibility,' I said.

'God,' she said. Then: 'Are you sure this isn't reverse psychology?'

'If it is, it's so subtle that even I'm not aware of it.' Then: 'Look. Why don't you think it over some more? You're not quite sure and we've still got twenty-four hours before we have to hand in our final list of witnesses.'

'It could ruin my life,' she said.

'I know.'

'Everywhere I go, people will recognize me.'

'Possibly.'

'And they'll think of me as a whore. That's the first thing that'll come to their minds. "There's that woman who testified for that rich guy she was having an affair with. She's a whore." ' Then: 'You know the funny thing?'

'What?'

'I came here to tell you I was going to do it. But now I'm not sure.'

'You weren't ready.'

'I wasn't?'

'Huh-uh. If you were really ready, you'd think of only one thing.'

'I would?'

'Yes. What your son said. The difference between right and wrong. You'd be willing to tell the truth.'

'Oh God, now I feel like a real shit.'

'You're not a shit at all. You're afraid and you'd be crazy not to be.'

'But if I really cared about right and wrong, about—'

'—telling the truth—'

'—then I'd—'

'—go ahead and agree to testify.'

'Oh, shit,' she said.

'What?'

'You know what I'm going to do?'

'What're you going to do?'

'I'm going to testify.'

'Great. I really appreciate this and so will everybody else involved in the case.'

'But they are going to call me a whore, aren't they?' she said, shaking her head miserably. 'They are going to call me a whore, right?'

I nodded.

'Well, I'll just have to live with it.'

Then she was gone. Out the door of my office.

I was just starting to turn back to my desk, when she peeked in again and said, 'I'm sorry. I just can't do it. I really can't.'

Then she was gone. For good.

A few hours later, on my way home, I decided to pick up the crosstown and visit the Wilsons.

The sweeping drive up the side of the hill was dark by now, the trees lining the drive filling with the cries of birds settling in for the night. For a moment, caught between opposing stands of trees, I felt blissfully alone. No more witnesses I had to talk into things. No more stepfathers to worry about. No more priests dead, or puzzling murders.

The house was dark.

No cars on the drive or near the garbage.

No sounds except the vague throb of the house itself, electricity and plumbing.

I was just about to walk up to the front door when I noticed the dark drops on the sidewalk.

Somebody had spilled something.

I knelt down, daubed a finger to one of the drops. Still warm, whatever it was.

I took out a penlight and shone it on my daubed finger.

Red. Blood.

I backtracked, bent old-man over so that my penlight could

214

pick out the drops. A raccoon squatted next to a carefully manicured flower bed, watching me.

The blood drops led all the way to the garage.

I followed them to the second door in the middle. I swung the door up and walked inside.

The blood was heavier here, splotches of it now.

Cars were on either side of me. The center stall was empty.

I felt a tightness in my chest and a coldness in my belly. Somebody had been injured, maybe even killed, and then taken away.

I thought about what Gilhooley had told me, Ellie Wilson liquidating all her assets over the past months.

Had she killed her husband, or had he killed her?

Or was there a third person here – the killer – who had forced them into the car?

There were too many possibilities.

Hearing something, I froze.

Clicked off my penlight.

Darkness. Sweaty darkness. Cold sweat.

Heart hammering. Mouth dry. A slight tic in my left eye.

Listening.

A clicking noise. And then I smiled, seeing the collie walking across the width of the drive, his golden and white fur pure in the moonlight. The clicking had been his nails on the concrete.

The collie went on into the night, and I followed the blood back to the front door. I shone my light on the door. Found a smudge of blood on the golden door knob. Took out my handkerchief and tried to turn the knob. Locked.

I went back to my car and called the police on my cellular phone. Asked for Detective Holloway.

'She's gone for the day,' a detective said.

'I'd like to have her home number if I could.'

'Sorry.'

I explained who I was, and he said, 'I can ask her to call you.'

I left my cell-phone number. Less than a minute later, she

called me back. 'Who is this?' She sounded annoyed.

'This is Payne,' I said. 'Something's going on.'

'Where are you?'

I told her where. And I told her what I'd found.

'I'll call the station. And keep an ear out. What's your phone number again?'

I gave her the cell phone and my home phone.

'You sound better tonight.'

'Yeah, I haven't sneezed practically all day.'

'Maybe it's over.'

'Yeah.' Then, 'Payne?'

'Uh-huh.'

'Bob Wilson's starting to look more and more like our boy,' she said.

'Yeah,' I said, 'that's kind of what I was thinking. At least, it would be if I could have thought of any reason for him to kill Tawanna Jackson and Ronald Swanson.'

'Yeah, but you don't *know* there's a connection. You just think there is.'

'And Michael Grady.'

'What are you talking about? That was an accidental drowning. I caught the squeal.'

'Maybe it was.'

'Hell, it *was*. So imagine, Ellie and the priest making out, Bob gets jealous, he kills the priest. And then tonight he and his wife have some kind of confrontation.'

'Yeah.'

'Happens all the time, Payne.'

'Yeah, it does.'

Maybe she was right.

'I'll call you if somebody finds them, all right?'

'Great. I appreciate it.'

Then she sneezed.

I cradled the phone, put the car in gear, and was just ready to start down the drive, when I heard the scream. I couldn't tell which direction it came from. Somewhere in the woods that sloped down the western side of the large hill.

The scream came again.

I dug my Luger and my flashlight out of the glove compartment, and got out of the car. I also grabbed the cell phone.

I jogged over to the head of the woods and listened. No more screams. No sounds except natural ones.

I clicked on my flashlight and started into the woods. This was an alien nocturnal world, alive with animals who watched me but whom I couldn't see, only sense. I followed a narrow path that wound downhill. I ducked innumerable branches, tripped over a few buried rocks, and twice took dead-end offshoots of the trail. The trees were only a few weeks into spring bloom but they were leafy enough to make seeing past them impossible. The loam smelled rich and heady.

The trail grew narrower and narrower as I reached the jack pines whose boughs slapped me eagerly. The Brothers Grimm wrote beautifully of dim dark woods. They would have loved this stretch of forest.

A sound. Faint. Uncertain.

I stopped. Cold sweat was now hot sweat. I was out of breath.

The sound again. Then I recognized it: a woman crying.

The path wound eastward now, and then dipped sharply. I saw the narrow creekbed below, and then I angled my flashlight to the left and I saw the woman lying next to the creekbed. Dead pieces of wood and dried leaves crackled as I walked, my light playing on branches and boughs impossibly vivid against the surrounding darkness.

I reached her moments later.

She kept her face down but I put my hand under her chin and forced her to look at me.

Someone had hit her pretty hard. Her left eye was puffy and red. She was going to have a black eye by the morning.

But her nose was my chief concern. It was bloody and possibly broken.

'What happened?' I said.

She was sweaty and dusty and disheveled from running

through the woods, her long-sleeved fuchsia blouse torn and dirty. Her wheat-coloured jeans showed a number of blotchy grass stains.

'You were going to leave him, weren't you?'

She nodded, sniffling.

'That's why you were liquidating all your holdings?'

Another teary nod.

'He found out about it?'

'Yes,' she said. She touched a hand to her bloody nose. 'He found out about it and started drinking when he got home from jail. His lawyer made bail. When I came in tonight, he was waiting for me.' She started crying again. 'I've never seen him this scary. He beat me up and then dragged me out to the car. I think he was going to take me out into the country and kill me, I really do. But I managed to run away, down here. He's out driving around looking for me.'

The dead leaves lining the creekbed smelled sweetly of death. In the summer, the woods were a playground for all animals; in the fall and winter, they were a coffin.

She said, 'I think he killed Father Daly.'

'Yeah,' I said. 'I was thinking that myself.' That he had. Or that she had.

'I think he was the one who pushed me when I was leaving Father Daly's office the last time I was there.'

'Pushed you?'

'Somebody was in the shadows at the top of the stairs. They pushed me. I suppose they thought I'd fall down the steps and hurt myself.'

'You couldn't see the person?'

'No. He ran down the corridor in the darkness. But I've always thought it was Bob. It'd be like him to sneak up to Father Daly's office and listen at the door.'

'You remember when this was?'

'The sixth of last month. He said he was at a poker game at Mike Timmins' place. I didn't believe him. Why?'

'Just wanted to know. No special reason.'

I took my cell phone from my jacket pocket and called

the police. I told them to send a car out to the Wilsons' immediately.

'I'm afraid to see him again,' she said. 'I thought I had it planned so carefully, too. I didn't think he'd find out till it was too late.'

'Why'd you show up at the police station last night if you were planning to leave him?'

She shook her head, then touched her hand again to her nose. 'I felt sorry for him. None of this would've happened if I hadn't gotten involved with Father Daly. I didn't want to leave him and feel guilty about it. I wanted to walk away clean. So I hired Harry Solomon.'

She looked at me. 'You have to understand, I don't hate my husband. I feel sorry for him. I don't want to see him spend the rest of his life in prison – but I don't want to spend the rest of my life with him, either. That would be *my* prison.'

'C'mon,' I said, getting up off my haunches. 'I'll walk you to the house.'

It took us fifteen minutes to get back to the house, with me half-carrying her. When we got there, three patrol cars were parked in a semi-circle, headlights all trained on the front door where Bob Wilson stood. His hair was mussed, some of his wife's blood showed on the front of his white shirt, and he was weaving back and forth, as if he were about to collapse.

'Just come on out, Mr Wilson,' one of the uniformed men said. 'Nobody's going to hurt you.'

'What for? I didn't do anything.'

Ellie looked at one of the cops and said, 'He was trying to kill me.'

'Kill you?' Bob said. And laughed angrily. 'Kill you? Babe, if that's what I had in mind, I would've done it a long time ago. Tonight I was just trying to make you come back to your senses. Leaving me may sound good now, but you wait a few months. You'll get lonely. You'll see. We belong together. We really do.'

He started weeping.

There was no warning. His head dropped, he brought a

219

big hand up to his face, and he began weeping.

The sound was startling. Even the cops were intimidated by it. You could see them shrink a little, very uncomfortable. You don't often hear a man sob so openly. We haven't trained ourselves in the art of crying and consequently, we don't know how to do it. Even when we're alone, most of us don't cry very cathartically. Even alone we've got to be worried about violating the code of *machismo*.

He fell against the frame of the house, hands clinging to the outline of the door for support. But his grasp wasn't strong enough to support him. He started to sink to his knees.

Forgetting her ankle, she crossed the distance between them in moments, and then got her hands under his arms. She was much stronger than I'd expected. She helped him stand erect and then she slid her arm around his waist.

'I'd like to take him inside and fix him a drink and talk to him a few minutes,' she said to the cop who'd done the talking.

'I don't know about that, ma'am.'

'I'll be fine. And he needs to calm down.'

'I'd like to send somebody in with you.'

'Then my husband won't talk. I know him, believe me.' Then, 'Tell them, Payne.'

'She'll be fine,' I said.

The uniformed cop walked over to me. He smelled sharply of after-shave. He was just starting to work on a pair of jowls.

'You're the one who called in?'

'Right.'

'This was supposed to be an emergency.'

'I don't think it is, any more.'

'We're supposed to take him down to the station.'

'Right.'

He leaned in. 'He's the killer, the way everybody figures.'

'He may be. I'm not sure yet.'

'I hate the hell to send her in there with him.'

'She'll be all right.'

'It's my ass if she isn't.' He smiled at me. He had a savvy, wise face. 'And then it's gonna be *your* ass, Payne.'

'That's the part I'm not crazy about. When it gets around to being my ass.'

He nodded and walked off, over to where the Wilsons stood in the doorway.

He reasoned with them like a referee before a prize fight. They could be inside only so many minutes. The front door was to be left open. And if Detective Holloway showed up and climbed all over this cop's ass, they were probably going to be forced back outside on the spot.

Seven minutes, he gave them.

Ellie and Bob Wilson disappeared through the doorway.

I thanked the cop in charge again, and then walked over to my car. I looked up at a second-floor window and saw three children looking down at us in apprehension. Poor kids.

As I was driving away, my cell phone beeped.

iii

As I swept down the hill, I passed a number of people standing in the darkness, staring up the hill like religious pilgrims. The truth they sought was an explanation for all the flashing red emergency lights staining the night sky.

I picked up the cell phone.

'She's called again,' Jean said. Jean was Brad Doucette's personal secretary. 'This Bernice woman. Three times in an hour. I thought I'd better tell you.'

'She say what she wanted?'

'No. Just that she had something very important to tell you.'

'She leave a number?'

'Yes.' She gave me the number.

'Why're you at the office so late?'

'Because I'm a salaried worker. If I was an hourly worker, Brad would never have me stay this late. You know how tight he is.'

'Brad tight? C'mon. I don't believe that.' I laughed.

I told Jean goodnight and then punched in the numbers she'd given me.

The line was busy.

A few minutes later, my cell phone buzzed.

'I've been trying to get hold of you,' Felice said, sounding happy to talk to me. 'Guess what happened?'

'What happened?'

I felt ridiculously good about being in her graces again, however temporary that might be.

'You know that Beverly Wright woman you were having so much trouble getting to testify?'

'Right.'

'Well, she called here. Vic answered the phone. He said you weren't here, but she just started talking anyway. She told everything and then just kept going back and forth. "Should I testify or shouldn't I testify?" And guess what?'

'What?'

'Vic convinced her to do the right thing.'

'He did?'

Then Vic was on the line. 'You owe me an airplane ride, Robert. She said she'd be deposed any time you tell her.'

'That's fantastic, Vic. Thanks a lot.'

'He's picking up the tab at the hospice and he's thanking *me*? Can you believe this guy, Felice?'

Then she was back on the line. 'It'll be great to see you tonight, Robert. Get here as soon as you can.'

'As soon as I can,' I said, thinking of all that was swirling around me. 'As soon as I can.'

After hanging up, I decided to try Bernice again. Still busy.

As I sat at a stoplight, I felt a kind of lethargy settle in. A light rain had begun to fall.

I wheeled into a convenience store and bought a giant paper cup of coffee and a large donut with a lot of food dye slathered across it.

I sat in the parking lot eating it.

Every minute or so, I tried Bernice's number.

When I finished my donut, I decided to check the number I was dialing. I took a phone book from the back seat.

The number was correct.

I tried again.

Busy.

I looked at the address. It was only about two miles from

here – a few minutes' trip. If what she had to say was so important, then it was probably worth me stopping by and hearing it in person.

Bernice lived in a tidy white bungalow that looked homey and inviting in the fog and rain of this night.

A light shone deep within the house. The kitchen, I suspected. Otherwise the place was dark.

A new Chevrolet sedan was parked in the drive.

I pulled in behind it and went up to the back door.

I knocked.

A neighborhood dog barked.

A baby cried somewhere.

I knocked again.

At first, I heard the sound only faintly, and I did not recognize it for what it was.

It was familiar in some respects, and yet not familiar at all in others.

I knocked for a third time.

The night smelled of cold rain and mud.

The sound again. This time, I identified it immediately. Weeping.

I reached down and tried the back door. Locked. Most likely with a latch inside.

I could snap it if I tugged on it hard enough, but I decided to try the front door first.

Walking along the edge of the drive, the only illumination a street-light lost to fog and rain, I stepped in a puddle deep enough to reach the top of my oxfords. Great.

I went up the three small front steps and knocked on the door. No answer.

I didn't expect to find the door unlocked – but it was.

I nudged it open and went inside. House smells. Warmth. Cut flowers. Cooking. Air freshener.

The room was junked up. Furniture had been overturned, the cushions on the couch pulled out and hurled on the floor.

Somebody had been looking desperately for something.

'Hello,' I called out.

No response.

'Hello.'

I walked through the living room and the dining room toward the sound that still faintly erupted every few moments. The weeping.

When I reached the kitchen, I found him, bent over Bernice's body, sobbing. Somebody had smashed in the side of her head. Blood stained the gray hair.

She lay rigid, displayed much as she would be in her coffin, even to her hands lying across her chest.

The man bent over her was slight and bald with freckles on his pate. He wore a white shirt and dark slacks. His shoes were Hush-Puppies.

'Oh honey, oh honey,' he sobbed, rocking back and forth on his heels, as if in rhythm to music that only he could hear.

He seemed startled to see me. He was so lost in his grief, he hadn't heard me knocking.

I helped him up. He rose in reluctant sections, up off his knees to his haunches, and then off his haunches to his legs.

He looked utterly baffled, even a bit insane.

'She isn't really dead, is she?'

Then he started crying again.

There wasn't anything I could say.

I helped him gently across the room to a kitchen table and sat him down. When he started to get up, I eased him back into his chair.

I began to search through the cupboards, opening and slamming doors until I found what I was looking for. At another time, I'd probably stop to admire all the handiwork. The appliances were all shiny new, there was a huge butcher block island in the center of the kitchen, and the cabinets showed the skill of real carpentry.

I grabbed a couple of glasses and carried everything to the table. I sat down across from him and poured each of us a good portion of his Black & White scotch.

'Did you call the police?'

'What?'

The baffled look again, as if he'd never heard the language I was speaking.

'Did you call the police?'

'Oh,' he said. 'No.'

'Drink your scotch.'

'What?'

'Your scotch.' I nodded to the glass in front of him. 'Drink it.'

'Oh.'

He drank. His hand was shaking so badly, I thought he was going to drop his glass. Some of the shaking was probably due to Parkinson's, but not much.

'When was the last time you talked to your wife?'

This time, he didn't say 'What?' he just stared at me.

'Listen to me. You need to help me so I can help you.'

'She's dead, isn't she?'

'Yes, I'm afraid she is.'

He broke again. There was no helping him for some time. I got up and fetched him several squares of Bounty paper towels so he could blow his nose.

'This doesn't make any sense,' he said, sounding sane for the first time.

'Maybe it does. Bernice was on to something. I'm not sure what it was – not yet.'

'You're the private investigator she told me about.'

'Right.'

'I've been out of town the last two days. I'm a salesman. I sell pizza ovens. But I call Bernice every night from the road, of course. And she told me about you.'

'Where would Bernice hide things?'

' "Things?" '

'Valuables.'

'Oh.'

He had slipped back into withdrawal. Every half minute or so he'd explode with a sob. And then he'd stop himself. Just sit there and stare at the table.

'Take another drink.'

'I'm not much of a drinker.'

'Take one, anyway.'

'Maybe I should.'

He choked on it and spent the next two minutes coughing. I didn't like pushing him this hard in these circumstances but I didn't have much choice.

'Where would Bernice hide something valuable?'

The withdrawn look again.

'I need you to listen to me.'

'Listen to you?'

'I'm asking a question. Do your best to answer it, all right?'

'Question.'

I sighed.

'Please look at me.'

After a long moment, he raised his gaze to my face.

'Are you listening now?'

'Yes.'

'Where would Bernice hide something valuable?'

'The safe.'

'The safe?'

'Sure. The wall safe in our TV room.'

Then he noticed what I was afraid he'd notice. When he'd bent over her, some of her blood came off on his white shirt.

He looked at it now in horror.

'Oh, my Lord,' he said. And immediately got out of his chair and started to walk back to her body.

I grabbed him and pushed him back down in the chair.

I took one of the squares of paper towels and handed it out to him. But then he slapped his hand over his mouth and I could see that he was going to vomit all over himself if I didn't move quickly.

I got him to the sink. Barely. He was throwing up before his stomach even pressed against the cabinet that held the double sinks of stainless steel.

I held him the way you'd hold a little kid vomiting and when he was done, I washed his face with a paper towel soaked in dish soap and then I took him back to his seat at the kitchen table.

'Drink up.'

'That's what made me throw up.'

'No, it isn't. The drink'll help you.'

He looked skeptical but he drank anyway.

I said, 'I need to get into that safe as soon as possible. Do you know the combination?'

'Sure.'

I could see that the vomiting had returned him to reality. Permanently, I hoped.

'I inherited this house from my father. He came through the Depression so he always saved something out of every paycheck and put it in the safe here at home. Didn't trust banks much.'

'I need you to open the safe.'

'I'm not handling this very well, Mr Payne. I'm sorry.'

'You're handling it a hell of a lot better than I would,' I said.

'Really?'

'Absolutely.' I'd stayed in bed for whole days following the death of my wife. Body and soul alike had shut down. 'We need to hurry.'

He nodded and stood up. I noticed how he carefully avoided looking down at his wife's body. He was a little stronger now but not that much stronger.

He led me out of the kitchen and down a hall. There were two bedrooms facing each other across the hall. At the rear of the bungalow was a long narrow room.

A large-screen TV dominated the west wall. Two three-shelf bookcases were pushed together, filled with what looked to be Book Club bestsellers. There were two leather recliners facing the TV.

The dainty patterns of the wallpaper and the nice sheer white curtains lent the room a cozy old-fashioned feel.

'We spent most of our nights in here,' he said.

He walked over to a print of a forest scene. It was a sentimental, idealized forest, the sort we daydream about escaping to.

A round wall safe lay flat against the wall.

From his shirt pocket, he took a pair of glasses, slipped them over his ears, and then proceeded to open the safe.

Given his condition, I thought that the procedure would take a while. It didn't. Two times to the left, one time to the right.

He reached inside.

He said, 'There's something in here that doesn't belong. Something – leather. I'm used to how everything feels.'

'I'd like to see it, if you don't mind.'

'Sure.'

He brought it out and looked at it and then showed it to me.

A leather-covered journal about the size of a hardbound book. I opened it and looked inside.

There was a name written in the upper right-hand corner.

'Is that why Bernice was killed?' he said.

'Yes,' I said, scanning some of the writing. 'Yes, I'm afraid it is.'

And my profile had been on the money.

Now I knew where I had to go. I couldn't wait around for the police.

iv

The rain stopped minutes later, then started again almost immediately – a silver slashing, and cold like most spring rains.

On the drive over to the rectory, I called the number Information had given me for Mike Timmins, with whom Bob Wilson had allegedly been playing poker the night his wife nearly got pushed down a flight of stairs outside Father Daly's office. According to Timmins, who seemed to be a bright, very forthcoming guy, Wilson had indeed played cards at his house that night, but had left early, by eight-thirty. Wilson would've had time to drive to the school and push his wife down the stairs.

I thanked him. That was the answer I had expected.

After parking at an angle in the darkened alley, I ran up the path between the rectory and church. I knocked hard on the side door of the rectory, huddled beneath the slight roof above the door, trying to keep from getting drenched by the rain.

No response at first. Then I saw a sleepy Jenny, yawning and stretching, coming up the basement stairs and squinting to see who was pounding. She looked young and vulnerable in her jammies and robe. It was Friday night, and not quite nine o'clock.

With the door open, I smelled the remnants of the night's meal.

Jenny covered her mouth for a final yawn. 'I'm sorry.'

'Is Father Ryan here, Jenny?'

She shrugged. 'I'm having a real hard period. I've been sacked out for the past couple of hours. Let me see who's here. You want to come inside?'

'No, I'll wait here.'

She pushed her face forward for a better look at me. 'You all right?'

'Yeah.'

'You don't look all right. You look kind of upset.'

'I'm fine. Really.'

She nodded, still trying to read my expression. 'I'll be right back.'

While I waited, I walked down the sloping sidewalk, back toward the alley and the large school that sat on the other side of it.

The windows, some bright with moonlight, others dark as secrets, peered down at me ominously. In one upstairs window I saw a dark shadow move quickly away from sight.

'Nobody's here,' Jenny said when she got back, this time with a pair of jeans and a sweater hastily pulled on. 'But I just remembered. Father Ryan hears confessions on Friday night, usually till nine-thirty or so. I've decided to attend. Sorry – I don't know where the Monsignor is.'

'No matter. Thanks, Jenny. Say, you couldn't lay hands on a key to Father Daly's office, could you?'

'His office? In the school?'

'I've never really checked it out. I'm hoping I'll find something there.'

'Like what?'

I smiled. 'That's the part I'm not sure about.'

'The key's right inside. I'll run and get it.'

Which she did. She handed it to me and said, 'If we hurry, I can walk to the school with you. I want to go to Confession before Father Ryan leaves the confessional. He makes me feel good.'

'No need for you to go with me,' I said. 'I'll be fine.'

We walked across to the church. I left Jenny there and went back across the alley to the school. One of the back doors was unlocked. I opened it and stood in the doorframe, shining my penlight inside.

The back door shouldn't have been unlocked. Not at this hour.

A long narrow hall faced me, lined with metal lockers. Classrooms lay on either side, very near this back door.

Familiar and poignant smells came at me: sweeping compound, chalk, wax on the wooden floors . . . For a moment, I was a boy again, sitting in class and hiding a Ray Bradbury paperback inside my math book.

I stepped inside. Listened.

Furnace and blower were suddenly noisy on the still, warm air. I remembered Bernice saying that Father Daly had his office upstairs in the far west corner.

I started walking down the corridor, the penlight in my left hand, my right hand very near the Luger in my jacket pocket.

The lockers had been dented down the years. Above them were group graduation photographs dating back to the twenties. I saw several decades' worth of hair and makeup styles flash by as I walked past the photos. It was like being in the deepest, darkest depths of a pyramid.

The stairs were around the first corner. I played my light up them. No untoward signs. The steps rose steeply and then turned sharply into another flight.

I kept playing my penlight on the steps as I climbed them, looking out for signs – blood, I suppose, the way I'd found it out at the Wilsons' tonight.

But I found nothing. Just dust and darkness.

The floor above was even darker. Jagged blue-white lightning glowed in the windows, casting the hall in an eerie blinding light, then vanished. Rain slanted coldly against the windows.

The lightning continued intermittently as I walked down towards the west end of the building. More photographs of long-dead people peered at me from above the lockers, their eyes seeming to follow me.

Father Daly's office door was ajar. It was an old-fashioned, pebbled-glass door with his name written neatly in black Magic Marker on a sheet of white typing paper: FATHER DALY.

Lightning again, this time illuminating an open-door classroom to my right. In the blue-white glow, I saw several rows of desks, the teacher's desk raised on a platform, and an American flag standing in a corner.

I walked up to Father Daly's door and peered around it, into the office itself.

This time there was no lightning to help me see. This time I had to rely on the thin beam of my penlight.

The priest's room was small and square. It contained two six-feet bookcases, a lumpy old couch, an easy chair, a desk, filing cabinet, and phone. Sparse and spartan. No doubt furnished with donations from parishioners wanting to unload some old furniture.

Then there was just the silent eeriness of the lightning again, and the shaking fury of the thunder.

I'd spent fifteen minutes reading through Father Daly's journal. Bernice must have taken it from Father Ryan's room earlier in the day, and when he found it gone, he knew exactly where to find it. He probably felt he hadn't any choice but to kill her.

The rain sounded loud and lonely as it beat coldly against the windows.

I didn't hear him come up to the doorway, didn't hear him take a few more steps into the office.

He was carrying a revolver but it was pointed at the floor.

'You found the journal, didn't you, Robert? Father Daly told Father Ryan that he'd written everything down in his journal – how Father Ryan was killing the confessors he couldn't prevent from doing evil. And that now he was going to turn the journal over to the police. That's why Father Ryan killed him.'

I watched my old friend in the doorway. He seemed

slightly stooped now . . . and fragile. I felt sorry for him. And I felt scared for him, too.

'You know, I'm in the journal, too. I didn't do any of the killing myself, I want you to know that, Robert. But I covered it up. I knew what Father Ryan was doing, but I was afraid it would destroy the parish after our sex scandal a couple of years ago. He promised me he'd stop, but he didn't. And, God forgive me, Robert, I let it go on!' My old friend hung his head in contrition.

I thought of what Steve had said that morning in Father Daly's motel room. 'There are some things we can forgive as priests that we can't forgive as men.' Father Ryan had repeated this during our conversation about forgiveness in the cafeteria. Now it all made grim sense.

'The people Father Ryan killed would've gone on doing the same things over and over and over,' Steve said calmly, 'and there wasn't anything anyone could do. Father Ryan felt he had to stop them.'

'You were the one Father Daly was arguing with out at the cabin,' I said.

'I'm sorry about this, Robert. I really am.' His smile was brief and grim. 'That's why I hired you – so I could see if Father Ryan had killed somebody else I didn't know about. I wanted to know everything.'

Then from the darkness of the hall, another voice: 'You didn't need to tell him anything.' It was Father Ryan.

I could see him outlined in the flickers of lightning that painted the walls silver every few minutes.

He held a gun on Steve.

'It's over, Father,' Steve said sadly. 'I should've turned you in long before now.'

'They deserved to die,' said Father Ryan. 'A pedophile, a wife-beater, a bully, a racist, a hooker who was spreading AIDS – how could I let them live? They'd just go right on doing it.'

'Give me the gun, Father,' Steve said gently. 'I'll see that you're treated well. I think hearing all those Confessions for so many years did something to you. Part of this is my fault, I'm sure.'

As he spoke, Steve moved closer and closer to him. And when he was very close, he said, 'Give me the gun now, Father.'

'No. I'm going to handle this my own way.'

Lightning flashed again just as Father Ryan made to move away and walk back down the hall.

Steve reached over and grabbed the priest's gun. And then spun him around, so that the two men were facing each other.

I don't think Father Ryan actually meant to do it, but that is irrelevant now. As soon as he was facing Steve, the priest tried to jerk out of Steve's grasp. And that's when the gun went off.

The explosion was loud and terrible in the rain-hissing night.

Father Ryan cried out something I couldn't understand. And then I heard him running away, his footsteps echoing in the darkness.

I didn't give a damn about Ryan any more. Not at the moment, anyway.

I went over and knelt down next to Steve. I could see that the wound was high in his chest, very near the heart. The pain was so bad, he was crying.

'Oh man, I should be a lot braver than this,' he said, obviously embarrassed that he was letting the pain get the best of him.

'I'm going to get an ambulance.'

Steve said, 'You always had more guts than I did, Robert. You would've turned him in a long time ago.'

'You were trying to protect the parish.'

'Or my own ego,' he said. Then he moaned again. 'I let everybody down, Robert. I really did.'

There was nothing dramatic about his passing. He stopped talking and his eyes closed. He smelled pretty bad suddenly. His bowels had given out.

I squatted on my haunches and looked at him for a long

time. I'd always envisioned him as the contemporary version of the country priest. I think that's how Steve wanted to see himself, too. But I'd been wrong. He was a lot more compli- cated than that. He'd been a good man, but by no means a perfect one.

I was sure as hell going to miss him.

I stumbled over to the phone and called Detective Holloway on her cell phone. She was, she said, already on her way.

The church was empty, echoing with the night. The smell of incense and the play of the votive candles lent the nave the feeling of a large cold cave.

I walked quickly down the center of the church, pew past empty pew. I saw nobody, heard nothing.

I raised my eyes and looked up at the choir loft. Shadow upon shadow darkened the loft until it was impossible to see anything but empty blackness.

She cried out then.

The sound was muffled, but I recognized it for what it was. And who it was. *Jenny*. She was just ahead of me, clutched in the iron grip of the murdering priest.

Father Ryan had hit her, temporarily knocked her uncon- scious presumably, giving him time to come over to the school and track me down. I could just see the upper part of her face – it was black and blue. Now Jenny was coming in handy. He had himself a hostage.

Then Jenny and Father Ryan had disappeared into the gloom of the vestibule.

A voice in the darkness. 'I'm taking her up there with me, Mr Payne. She needs to die just as the rest of them did. I used to think there was hope for her, but there isn't. I saw her with you. She's a whore. A whore!' Then: 'Stay back, Mr Payne. Or I'll shoot her right here.'

I stopped.

A door opened.

Shuffling, scuffling feet . . .

Another muffled cry.

A long moment of shadows and silence. I wanted to help her, but I had no doubt that the priest would kill her if I tried.

Sirens then, in the rain and gloom of fog. Coming closer, closer.

When I heard their feet scuffling on the bell-tower steps, I followed them, walking silently carefully towards the tower door.

He was going to take her up to the very top of his beloved eyrie . . .

I tried not to think about what he might do when he got her up there. In my time, I've seen a lot of human bodies that have fallen against the unforgiving pavement below. I once saw the sad, shattered remains of a four-year-old girl smashed against the ground – twelve stories down from the window she'd fallen out of.

I glanced behind me. Through the stained glass on either side of the double doors of St Mallory's I could see the bleak lights of police cars and other emergency vehicles.

I eased open the door to the tower. Stepped on the bottom stair. Listened.

A chilly draft swept down from the tower.

I heard them then, far far above me. He must be very close to the bell itself by now, I thought.

She whimpered.

The sharp, slashing noise of a slap.

Another whimper.

The double doors were thrown back. There stood Detective Holloway surrounded by half a dozen cops in rain-drenched jackets. They each held a shotgun.

Detective Holloway walked over to me and said, 'Where's Father Ryan?'

I nodded at the bell-tower stairs. 'He's got himself a hostage. A girl who works at the rectory.'

'Great. Just what we need.'

'He may listen to me.'

'No offense, Payne, but why would he listen to you?'

'Because maybe I understand him a little bit.'

'You do?'

I shook my head. 'I didn't say I approved of him. I just said I understood him a little.'

The scream stopped both Holloway and me from saying any more.

I ducked my head into the stairwell and looked up the long, cold shadowy steps.

'Let's see if he'll let me go up there,' I said.

I started up the crazily winding stairs. Every few steps, I heard the wooden staircase make small, but very clear noises. I assumed Father Ryan could hear them, too.

I moved one very self-conscious step at a time.

The shaft got colder the higher I went. I smelled wood and dust and the cold rain. I was climbing half-blind. The only light was a pale luminescence from the tower itself, though by now I assumed Detective Holloway was probably blasting all sorts of emergency light up from the vehicles surrounding the church.

Another moan of pain.

Then Detective Holloway on a speaker system. 'Father Ryan, we don't want to make this situation any worse than it is. Please let the girl go and then turn yourself over to the police. We're not going to hurt you, Father. We have only the best of intentions.'

A strangled cry. I pictured him with his hand clamped over Jenny's pale, bruised face.

Inch by chilly, shadowy inch, I made my way around the final twist of the tower stairs.

The moment I rounded the bend, I saw the rectangle cut of the tower floor, where the stairs ended.

There was no sign of either of them. I imagined that he was holding her very near one of the openings in the tower, threatening to push her to the pavement far, far below should anybody try to rush in and save her.

I had to be careful. I could very easily get Jenny killed.

I climbed four of the last six steps and eased my head up a few inches above the floor.

The priest had shoved Jenny into one of the openings in the

239

tower. A simple push would send her crashing to her death.

I took one more step.

Rain in the form of a cold spray splashed across my face.

I took the final step.

I stood on the floor of the tower, the bell huge and imposing.

'We want you to understand,' Detective Holloway said through her horn. 'You won't be harmed, Father. You have a lot of friends here tonight.'

In a few minutes, she'd probably turn it all over to a negotiator trained in dealing with these situations.

He heard me then.

I'd made no noise whatsoever, but suddenly – as if he'd become aware of me telepathically – he turned toward me, Jenny still in his grip.

He looked crazed, his face a mask of frenzy and despair. His free hand held the cold blue steel of a .38 service revolver.

'I'm sorry I killed the Monsignor,' he said. 'He was a decent man.'

'Yes, he was. And Jenny's a decent woman. Why don't you let her go down the stairs?'

'Oh, that'd be real smart, wouldn't it? Then what, Payne? I just wait for them to come up here and get me?'

'They're going to get you anyway,' I said gently. 'Why not let Jenny go before she gets hurt, too?'

'They deserved to die, Payne.'

'I think they probably did.'

I took a step forward.

'What're you doing?' he asked.

'I just don't want to fall down the opening there.'

'Stay right where you are, Payne.'

As he said that, Jenny's gaze traveled to the hand holding the gun. While he had his hand gripped tight on her mouth, he wasn't paying attention to the right hand, which was dangling free. I assumed she was going to make a grab for the gun. This was a great risk, but right now there didn't seem to be any other opportunity.

A new voice came over the horn below – a man's voice,

deep and intelligent and full of calculated compassion.

This was the negotiator.

I'd heard this spiel many times before, so I didn't pay any attention to the words, just the tone.

The voice was disturbing Father Ryan. He kept looking over his shoulder, as if the negotiator might be scaling the tower all the time he was talking.

I was watching Jenny's face. She was trying to squirm her way out of the priest's grasp, but having no luck.

I said, 'Father—'

She moved then. She wasn't trained. She wasn't even very good at it, all awkward, girlish zeal, but she did all the right things. Kicked him hard in the shin and then managed to get her hand around his wrist and push the gun away from pointing at me.

He fired twice, but the bullets disappeared in the tower opening to my left.

Jenny bit his arm and forced him to let go of her just long enough for her to spin away. There wasn't much room for her to run. She took three long steps toward me. I grasped her hand, pulled her over to me, and pushed her behind me.

Father Ryan was frantic. He still held his gun and had it pointed at us, but now he was looking behind him every few minutes.

Did he suspect the police were going to pick him off with a sniper? Did he think there was somewhere to escape to?

'You're tired, Father. You're going to hurt yourself up here,' I said. 'And there's no reason for that.'

I took a step toward him. Then another.

'Stay there!'

'You're not going to shoot me, Father. You only killed Father Daly when he was going to turn you over. And you didn't mean to kill Steve at all.'

He glanced behind him again.

I'd noticed that for every step I took, he backed up one.

He was now no more than one or two paces from the edge of the tower opening directly behind him.

241

'You have to be careful, Father. You're going to hurt your-self like I said.'

This was my best chance and I wasn't sure if he'd take that final step. I had to be ready to grab him.

'Stay there,' he said again.

'Start down the stairs, Jenny,' I said.

'I'll stay here with you,' Jenny said from behind me.

'The stairs, Jenny,' I said. '*Now.*'

'She stays with us,' the priest said.

'Go, Jenny.'

She walked around me, glancing anxiously at the priest and his weapon.

'He's not going to hurt me?'

'Go.'

She finally did what I wanted her to, and started climbing down into the darkness below.

I looked at the night sky in the tower openings. With the searchlights playing against the heavy cloud cover, the night was an eerie and unnatural gray color.

'Are you all right?' I called down to Jenny.

'I'm fine,' she shouted up.

I looked at Father Ryan and then prepared myself.

Would he move instinctively, unconsciously, as he had done before?

I started forward.

'Stay right there!' he said.

But this time he didn't take a step back. He stood his ground.

'I want to help you, Father.'

'I don't need your help.'

I finished the rest of my step. 'I might have done the same thing you did, Father. Maybe I wouldn't have been able to handle it, either, hearing those things night after night in the confessional.'

I wasn't lying, either. How many stories about beating up black people or Jews or gays could you bear? How many stories of old ladies with crushed skulls, the few pennies of their life-savings taken by drugged-up punks? How many stories of children molested or murdered? Television has made us all witnesses to these acts, day in, day out. And the confessor has the even worse task of hearing of them in person. As a priest he could forgive; but as a man . . . Whether we want to admit it or not, we've all got vigilante impulses, every one of us. The thing is to control them . . .

'Let me help you, Father,' I said. 'Please.'

I slowly put my hand out, in the most unthreatening way I knew how. For a moment, I thought he might take it but then—

He didn't fall out of the tower, but he did lose his balance and start to grab the side of the opening. I lunged for him, getting hold of his shoulder. But, abruptly, in an almost serio-comic way, fat Oliver Hardy doing a pratfall, his left foot slipped off the edge of the tower opening and he started to fall. I grabbed his wrists, concentrating all my strength in my hands, supporting him as best I could. I was afraid he might pull me over with him.

Rain sprayed my face. The searchlights blinded me as they criss-crossed the tower. Meaningless words barked from the speaker horn below.

I could hear the cops pounding up the stairs.

Would they make it before my strength gave out?

'Just let me go, Payne,' Father Ryan said. 'It'll be better for everybody.'

'I can't do that, Father.'

Footsteps. Pounding, pounding, pounding up the stairs.

'They deserved to die, Payne,' he said. 'They really did.'

'That wasn't your decision to make, Father.'

'Maybe it wasn't, Payne. But this is.'

He turned his wrists inside my hands. And then he was free.

As I'd feared, his sudden movement jerked me forward. I had to grab onto the rough side of the opening to keep from falling myself.

I didn't want to watch his fall, but something made me.

Some dark voyeuristic impulse, I suppose.

Down, down, down he went, falling through the fog stained red by the emergency lights.

He didn't scream, but they did, the people below.

They screamed a whole lot.

Before I left the church, I stood in the back and said a prayer. For who or what, I wasn't sure. I just kept thinking of what Steve Gray had said to me once. That all great religions have at their center the same tenets: mercy and charity.

I kept thinking about that all the way back to my apartment in the soft, silent rain.

V

After we got Vic moved into the hospice, the three of us drove out to the small private airport I use.

Like Susan, Vic got the whole treatment – leather helmet, goggles, leather jacket, leather gloves – and he also got nearly an hour in the air on this warm sunny day.

Then we had lunch and did some last-minute shopping for things he'd need, and then we took him back to the hospice.

We walked him to the front door and Felice put her arms out and hugged him.

'You're sure a sweetheart,' he said.

Then he looked at me. 'Thank you for everything, Robert.'

In all the years we'd lived together, I'd never once shaken hands with him.

I thought of all those years I'd hated him, seen him as a buffoon who'd stolen my family life.

But I didn't see him as that any more. I didn't like him and never would. But I saw his decency now and his sadness.

I put my hand out. We shook.

'Well,' he said, 'guess I'll be getting inside.'

'Remember,' Felice said, 'we're taking you out for dinner two nights a week.'

He smiled with his store-boughts. 'You don't think I'm going to forget that, do you?'

I took Felice's hand as we walked to the car.

'I hear Ellie Wilson is getting a divorce,' she said.

'Where'd you hear that?'

'Your secretary.'

I smiled. 'I guess I should call the office more often.'

I performed one of my occasional acts of gallantry and held the door open for her. Then I walked around to my side and slid behind the wheel. I was just firing up the engine when she leaned over and kissed me. 'You did good,' she said.

I started driving us home.

'Maybe I'm finally growing up,' I said. 'About Vic, I mean.'

'Maybe,' she said. Then smiled. 'At least a little bit.'

Then she reached over and put her hand on my knee and said, 'I was really proud of the way you handled yourself back there, Robert.'

'Yeah,' I said, 'I guess I was kind of proud of me, too.'

Then I took her hand in mine and squeezed it.

'Thanks,' I said.

'For what?'

'You know for what, Felice,' I said. 'You know for what.'

And then we drove on home.